The Black Dog

'A short distance down the road, a narrow
lane led to a wooden door set in the wall
around the Wiltshaw estate. Since the
death of old Mr. Wiltshaw it had hardly
been used, and was now almost completely
overgrown with weeds and hedges that
formed a tangled, thorny arch, cutting out
the warmth of the sun.

   The children paused and glanced back.
The great clumps of cow parsley at the
mouth of the lane shut them off completely
from sight of the road.

   'We could be the only people alive,' said
Maeve.

   She had no sooner spoken when there was
an absolute eruption of movement in the
hedge beside them. For a moment, every
ghost story they had ever heard flashed
through their minds . . .'

Tony Hickey

The Black Dog

Illustrated by Terry Myler

ACORN BOOKS
The Children's Press

First published in 1985 by
The Children's Press
90 Lower Baggot Street, Dublin 2

This book is published with the financial
assistance of the Arts Council
(An Chomhairle Ealaíon), Dublin

ISBN 0 900068 93 0 cased
ISBN 0 900068 94 9 paper

Typesetting by Computertype Limited
Printed in Ireland by Mount Salus Press Limited

Contents

1 Holidays

The sun rose over the Wicklow mountains and spread its golden light across the great plain of Kildare.

In the vast grazing lands around the little town of Innisdara cattle stirred and fine horses galloped giddily, kicking out at the new day. But in the town itself nothing moved. The protective barrier of trees that gave the town its ancient name of Innisdara, the Island of Oak-trees, made it seem like a dark-green island in a sea of grass and ripening grain.

Gradually the sun rose higher in the sky, its rays touching the edge of the town, like a warm tide lapping against the shore. Slowly the town came to life.

Lying in her bed, Maeve Maguire knew exactly what each sound in the street below meant.

First there was Mr. Ryan taking down the shutters of his shop.

Then Mr. Kelly opened the side door of his pub and let out his five mangey-looking cats which, he insisted, were the best ratters in the county.

Then little Miss Grogan began to sweep her front doorstep, on which no dust was ever allowed to rest.

A while later, the Nolans would begin their daily task of trying to start their car. They would as usual be late for work at the quarry on the Hill of Allen.

Then the Brady brothers would back their van out on to the road and set off to finish the bungalow they were building close to Prosperous for a returned American.

Maeve could also picture the battered old school bus parked outside McGraths' battered old garage. If buses could dream it was surely dreaming of the fine rest it would have now that the school year had finished.

The smell of breakfast drifted upstairs, making Maeve realize how hungry she was. She jumped out of bed and scrambled into a pair of green cords and her favourite tee-shirt with the words 'I'm a Genius' on it. The first time her father had seen it, he'd said very dryly, 'Chance would be a fine thing.'

He often said things that he hoped would be funny in that dry way. Maybe it had something to do with being a solicitor. Maeve had read that the law is a 'very dry profession'. Certainly the law books in his office looked very dry and serious.

'Still,' Maeve thought, 'that's not his fault.' She ran a comb through her hair, tied it back with a red ribbon, dashed into the bathroom, washed her face, hands and teeth and bounced downstairs.

'Such a racket!' her father said.

'Maeve, The Space Walker,' her brother Joe said.

But the nickname never worried Maeve. She was quite proud of being able to move so fast even though she was small for a twelve-year-old while Joe, who at eleven was taller and bigger than she was, was much slower. Of course doing things quickly could sometimes end in disaster.

The worst time had been last Easter. Having got up early to give her parents their breakfast in bed, she had tripped over a mat in the hall and landed with a crash and a scream that had brought everyone rushing downstairs. Although they had been delighted that she had not been hurt, Joe couldn't resist saying, 'Trust Maeve, the Space Walker, to start the day with a bang!'

She knew he had meant it as a joke just as she would call him 'Joe, the Speckled Thrush', because of the mass of freckles on his face. They were really very good friends, which was just as well since, apart from a few babies, they were the only pre-teenagers in Innisdara.

As the first slices of toast popped up out of the toaster, the post arrived. Mr. Maguire flicked through the letters quickly: 'Bills, bills, bills!' Then he paused and looked at a long white envelope. 'Ah, at last! I've been waiting for this one.'

Mr. Maguire read the letter twice before he spoke. 'I'll have to go to Dublin today,' he said to Mrs. Maguire, 'and you'd better come with me. It's about the Wiltshaw estate.'

The Wiltshaw estate was one of the largest in the district, with a fine Georgian house standing in the middle of parkland surrounded by a high wall. Mr. Maguire, like his father before him, was the solicitor for the whole place.

'Has a buyer been found for it then?' Mrs. Maguire asked.

'That's what they want to see us about.'

'I'd hate to see the estate split up and divided after being in the one family for so long.'

'Maybe it's been too long with that family, if that family doesn't appreciate it,' Mr. Maguire replied.

Maeve and Joe knew that he was referring to Julia Wiltshaw who had inherited the estate when her father had died four years before. She lived in Dublin now and seemed to have no interest in the house and the land, apart from selling it for as much money as possible.

'I'll get the files out after breakfast.' Mrs. Maguire knew as much about her husband's practice as he did, and her ambition was to become a solicitor herself. 'Can the children come to Dublin with us?'

'Only if they want to spend the first day of their holidays sitting around offices. They certainly can't go wandering around the city by themselves.' Mr. Maguire didn't care much for cities.

'We can go wandering around the countryside then,' Maeve said. 'We can take a picnic.'

'A picnic?' Mr. Maguire repeated the word as though Maeve had said something rude. He hated picnics as much as he hated cities, insisting they were for people of no fixed address. Mrs. Maguire, however, loved the idea, thinking of how tidy the kitchen would stay if the children did not have lunch there. She said, 'There's a bit of cold chicken in the fridge and some tomatoes and apples. I can shop in Dublin and we'll have a proper meal this evening.'

And so it was settled. Thirty minutes later Mr. and Mrs. Maguire had departed for the city. Ten minutes after that Joe and Maeve were closing the front door behind them.

'But where are we going?' Joe asked.

'To see if we can find Finn's Way,' Maeve answered.

'What's Finn's Way?'

'Miss Neilan in school was telling us that Finn MacCool and the Fianna used to hunt around the Hill of Allen. You know who the Fianna were?'

'Of course I do. They were the special soldiers of the High King of Ireland, but I never heard of them having

10

anything to do with the Hill of Allen.'

'Well it seems that they did. They even had a fort there and there is supposed to have been a road that went from the Hill of Allen to the Hill of Tara.'

'The Hill of Allen is miles away.'

'Not if we cut through the Wiltshaw estate. I got the idea listening to Dad and Mam talking just now. The estate will bring us out almost at Robertstown. We can have our picnic by the canal.'

Miss Grogan had finished sweeping her doorstep and was cleaning her bedroom window as the children set off down the short main street. She waved a duster at them. Maeve waved back but Joe blushed as he always did

when he saw Miss Grogan. She thought he had a lovely speaking voice and every chance she got she would make him read a poem from a leather-bound book that she kept on the mantlepiece in her front room. She particularly liked sentimental poems and her very favourite one began:

> Oh, my love is like a garden
> Covered o'er with snow.
> And, until you help me thaw it out,
> Nothing sweet will grow.

If Maeve was there when Joe was reading she would sit in a corner where Miss Grogan couldn't see her and roll her eyes and make kissing movements with her lips. Joe was always terrified that Miss Grogan would catch her at it and think they were both making fun of her. But now, thank goodness, it was too early in the day for poetry. But even if Miss Grogan had been in the mood to have Joe read aloud, Joe did not give her the opportunity to ask. Walking as fast as he possibly could, he looked neither to the left nor the right until the main street of Innisdara was behind him and he was out in the countryside.

Maeve laughed, not just because she knew how Joe felt about reading to Miss Grogan but also because it was so terrific to think of no more school for so many weeks and equally terrific to have the sun shining and the empty road stretching out in front of them.

It was hard to believe that only a few miles away there was a never-ending line of lorries and cars and buses and vans roaring along the new motorway, in and out of the city.

2 The Black Dog Appears

A short distance down the road, a narrow lane led to a wooden door set in the wall around the Wiltshaw estate. Since the death of old Mr. Wiltshaw the lane had hardly been used and was now almost completely overgrown with weeds and hedges that formed a tangled, thorny arch, shutting out the warmth of the sun.

When the children had walked only a short way down the lane, Maeve paused and said, 'It's as though we've come into a different world and a different season.'

They glanced back over their shoulders. The great clumps of cow parsley at the mouth of the lane cut them off completely from sight of the road. 'We could be the only people alive.'

She had no sooner spoken when there was an absolute eruption of movement in the hedge beside them. For a moment, every ghost story they had ever heard flashed through their minds. Then suddenly a black snout appeared through the tangled undergrowth and there was a faint keening to be heard.

'It's a dog,' Maeve said, 'caught in the hedge.' She dropped down on her knees and began to force the tangle of hedge apart. When the gap was wide enough a fine, big, black labrador with a beautiful silky coat and bright alert eyes crawled out into the lane. He shook himself several times and wagged his tail.

'You silly thing!' Maeve said. 'I hope you realize you gave us a terrible fright.'

'I wonder who he belongs to.' Joe touched the expensive red leather collar around the dog's neck but it had no identity disc on it.

The dog sniffed the air. He turned his head away from Joe and sniffed the air again. 'He's on to something,' Joe said. 'I wonder what it is.'

Suddenly Maeve knew what it was, but she was too late to prevent the dog from picking up the brown paper bag that she had dropped. 'It's my picnic that he's after!'

The dog stood there with the bag in his mouth. He looked so pleased and so pleading that Maeve had not the heart to refuse him. 'Oh, all right. If you're that hungry, you can have the chicken. Joe'll share his with me but I don't think you should eat the bag as well.'

She held out her hand and the black dog dropped the bag into it. 'Sit,' she said. The dog sat. 'He's been very well trained.'

The dog watched patiently while Maeve unwrapped the chicken. He accepted the piece she gave him with a gentle wag of the tail. But even as he swallowed it he went on alert again and dashed down the lane to the door in the wall. He listened. Then he began to bark furiously.

'He could well have heard his owner calling him,' Joe said, as he and Maeve hurried forward. 'Maybe his owner is inside the estate.' He shooed the dog to one side and tried the handle of the door but the door wouldn't budge. 'It's locked.'

'We could try the main gates,' Maeve suggested.

'Or, quicker again, have a look over the wall and see if there's anyone there. I'll give you a leg up.'

Maeve hesitated. Then she realized that Joe's suggestion was a sensible one. After all, he was too heavy for her to lift. Gingerly she allowed him to help her to reach for the top of the wall. She could feel him wobbling quite a bit and the dog had stopped barking to watch. But even standing on Joe's shoulders didn't allow Maeve to see into the estate.

'I'll have to sit on the wall.'

'Well, be careful you don't fall.'

'Of course I won't fall.' Yet somehow between hauling herself on to the top of the wall and trying to sit on it, she lost her balance, and to Joe's horror vanished from sight with a deafening scream like the one she had given when she had dropped the breakfast tray.

'Maeve ...?' Joe yelled. 'Can you hear me? Maeve ...?'

But there was no reply. Desperately Joe scanned the wall but there was no grip of any kind. 'What are we going to do?' Without meaning to, he had spoken to the dog.

The dog ran to the gap that Maeve had made in the hedge and barked. Joe understood. 'You want me to follow you? Is that it? O.K. Off you go.'

The dog scrambled through the hedge with Joe crawling after as best he could. His tee-shirt caught on a bramble and ripped but he had no time to worry about that.

The dog raced along, following the wall. Joe skidded to a halt in the front of a barred metal gate through which the parkland could be seen. 'I only hope it isn't locked as well.' Joe slipped his fingers through the bars and tried the bolt. It opened as easily as if it were in constant use.

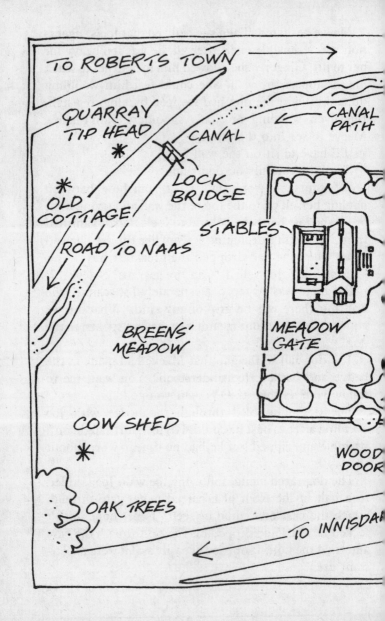

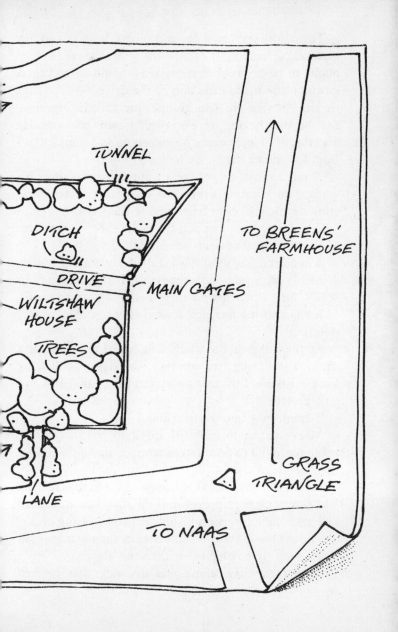

TUNNEL

DITCH

DRIVE

MAIN GATES

WILTSHAW
HOUSE

TREES

LANE

TO BREENS'
FARMHOUSE

GRASS
TRIANGLE

TO NAAS

The dog slipped past Joe and across the parkland but instead of heading towards the place where Maeve ought to be he went first towards the house and then swung back in the direction of the drive.

'Hey, where are you going?' Joe yelled, forgetting that he and the dog were on two different missions. He also forgot to look where he was going and went sprawling, face downwards, on to the ground.

'Well, I must say we are a right pair; me falling off walls, you tripping over your own feet!' Maeve was running towards him from among the trees.

'I wouldn't have tripped if I hadn't been so worried. Why didn't you answer when I called you?'

'I couldn't. My mouth was full of dry grass. Luckily, I landed on a pile of it, otherwise I might have been really hurt. But what on earth is the dog up to now?'

Joe got to his feet and looked to where Maeve was pointing.

At the edge of the ditch that edged the drive and drained it during bad weather, the dog was dancing backwards and forwards giving out little half-barks and half-growls.

'I think he's found something.'

Maeve began to walk towards him but had hardly taken more than a dozen steps when up out of the ditch a man began to rise.

Even at the distance that separated them, the children had a very clear impression of the man's pale haggard face and the expression in his deep-set, staring eyes.

The expression was a mixture of despair and anger at being seen by anyone other than the dog.

Indeed the dog alone was unaware that he had

revealed the man's hiding-place for he began to jump at the man, trying to lick his face.

Then he did the same kind of dance as when he had wanted to be followed by Joe.

The man climbed the rest of the way out of the ditch and half-ran, half-limped, after the black dog, towards the trees on the side of the parkland furthest away from the children.

Maeve shielded her eyes against the bright sunlight but it was impossible to make out if the man and the dog were standing watching them. Suddenly Maeve felt as she had while standing in the lane; that they were the only people left in the world. There was not a sound to be heard. Nothing moved. The trees so carefully planted two hundred years before, the grass, still carpet-like in spite of being neglected, seemed lost in a world of their own. The house was like some great stone monster whose window eyes could look for ever at the bright sun without blinking. Maeve shivered.

'You can't be cold in this heat,' Joe said.

'It all seems so strange,' Maeve said. 'And the way that man rose up out of the ditch! It was like Dracula rising out of the grave.'

'Dracula never comes out in the daylight,' Joe tried to sound cheerful but he knew exactly how Maeve felt. There *was* a strange feeling about the place. 'And as far as I know Dracula didn't have a dog.'

'Do you think that man owns the dog?'

'I do,' said Joe. 'And did you see the trouble he had running? I think he hurt his foot and that the dog went looking for help — only he expected the man to be at the house and not in the ditch.'

'The house?' Maeve stared at the house again. She was beginning to feel even more solemn and serious. 'Then he must have just left it when he heard me falling off the wall and you shouting. That must have been when he hid in the ditch.' She glanced towards the line of trees where they had last seen the man and the dog. 'Do you think he's still watching us?'

'I don't know,' Joe said. 'Should we go up to the house and make sure that everything is all right? After all, Dad is more or less responsible for the place. You're not afraid, are you?'

'Afraid of what? Of looking in the windows of an empty house? I was just thinking it's all a bit like a dream.'

'Except that we are wide awake. And we might have to do more than look in the windows.'

They had moved towards the drive now. The sun was out of their eyes and they could clearly see the front of the house. The great hall door was wide open!

3 The Mysterious Visitor

They walked quickly up the drive, glancing around occasionally, but there was no further disturbance of the parkland's strange stillness.

However, traces of recent movement on the gravel by the front steps convinced them that Joe had been right in suggesting that the man had been near the house.

They ran up the steps and looked inside. The entrance hall and the great staircase that curved to the upper floors looked the same as on the day that old Mr. Wiltshaw had been buried. It was as though his daughter, Julia, had only just that minute driven off after the funeral.

They crossed the hall and went into the dining-room. The shutters on one of the windows were open and the bright sunlight streamed in on the furniture, most of it covered, like coffins, with white dust-sheets. Over the fireplace there was a portrait of Mr. Wiltshaw as a young man. He looked proud and haughty, not at all like the kind old gentleman who used to call to see their parents.

Between a pair of matching sideboards, a door led into the kitchen. The children gazed in amazement at the tiled floors, the huge old-fashioned range and the tables that still seemed newly scrubbed in spite of the layer of dust on them. 'The whole downstairs of our house would fit in here,' Maeve said.

A flight of stairs was visible through a narrow archway. 'I'll bet that goes to the servants' bedrooms,' Joe said. 'I think now that we are here we should have a proper look around. I wonder why just one shutter in the dining-room was left open.'

The stairs, much narrower than the grand staircase, ran up through the back of the house. It was dark and gloomy with only one window on the top landing letting in daylight. From this window the children caught a glimpse of the stableyard and outhouses down below and, also, a splendid view across the countryside of the tower on the Hill of Allen and the canal shining like a diamond bracelet as it wound through the countryside.

The first of the bedrooms on the corridor off the landing had no furniture at all in it. The second one was a kind of dump-room, filled with cardboard boxes and bits of old carpet. But in the third bedroom, there was a small pine dressing-table, a chair, and a bed that looked as though it had recently been slept in.

'What was that?' Maeve went to the bedroom door to listen. 'I thought I heard someone downstairs. There it is again! Do you suppose that man followed us into the house?'

Joe felt the hairs on the back of his neck tingle but managed somehow to keep his voice steady. 'Well if he was watching us, he knows that we're here. We left the door of the dining-room open. He could easily guess that we came up through the house by the back stairs.'

'Which means we have to go down the front one! There's bound to be a door connecting this part of the house with the main part. Come on!' Maeve grabbed Joe by the arm and propelled him towards the one door that they had not so far opened.

On the other side, there was a carpeted corridor lined

22

with pictures and gilt wall-lights. In front of them, the children saw the elegant curve of bannister that marked the top of the grand staircase.

The carpet beneath their feet killed all sound of their footsteps, so they had no need to creep along. They looked down into the hall. There was no one there and the front door was still open wide.

Maeve and Joe gripped the bannister firmly. This was no time to risk tripping for, apart from the danger of being caught by that strange-looking man, to fall down so many stairs could really damage a person. All the same, they both jumped the last four steps and sped across the hall towards the sun-drenched front steps. They had just reached them when a voice yelled at them, 'Hey, hold on there! Where do you think you're going?'

The children turned around, amazed, for they recognized the voice as that of Mr. Gallagher, the retired postman of Innisdara. He was as surprised to see them as they were to see him. 'Well, what in heaven's name are the two of you doing here? You've put the heart crossways in me. I thought there was an intruder in the house.'

'There *is* someone in the house,' Joe moved further away from the front door and looked at the upstairs windows. 'We think he's actually living here.'

Mr. Gallagher's eyebrows shot up. 'Have you two been out too long in the sun?'

'It's true,' Maeve insisted. 'We saw the bed he's been using in one of the attic rooms.'

'That's MY bed,' Mr. Gallagher said. 'Did your father not tell you that I'm what you might call the care-taker of this place?'

The children shook their heads.

'After I retired from the post-office, I had plenty of spare time, and a place will get musty and damp without light and air.'

'Then it was you who opened the shutter in the dining room?' Joe asked.

'That's right.'

'And the front door too?'

'Yes. Any day that it's not raining, I open all the doors.'

'And there's no one else staying here?' Maeve's question startled the old man but without waiting for him to speak she added, 'We saw a man and a black dog wandering around the parkland.'

'A man and a dog? Now who the blazes could that have been? The two of you would recognize him if he was from Innisdara or anywhere around about. And how the devil did he get in here? In fact now that I think of it, how the devil did the two of you get in here? The gates are all locked.'

'The one over there at the meadow is only bolted. I came in that way.'

'There was a lock on it then last evening,' Mr. Gallagher said, 'for I took a short cut over to the Breens to make arrangements about the Macra na Feirme field day. The whole county will be going to it. I'm amazed the two of you aren't off to it too.'

'We forgot about it,' Joe said, 'and decided to try and find Finn's Way while the weather is fine.'

Mr. Gallagher sighed and shook his head. 'Now don't tell me young people still try to find that? Many's the summer day I spent looking for it when I was growing

24

up but I never found it. And indeed how could anyone, when the countryside it passed through has changed so much?' Then the worried look came back into his eyes and he squinted at the bright light that now was reducing the parkland to a blur. 'A man and a black dog, eh?'

'A tall, thin, very pale man,' Joe said.

'With longish black hair?'

'Yes,' said Joe. 'That's him.'

'A fellow fitting that description was here about ten days ago, enquiring about the trees. He was from a timber merchant.'

'Do you mean he wanted to buy the trees and cut them down?' Maeve was horrified at the idea. 'The place wouldn't be the same without them.'

'And I said as much to him. In fact I told him to go off about his business, that nothing was for sale around here.'

'But it's all for sale,' Joe said. 'Julia Wiltshaw wants to get rid of everything.'

'Then let the shame of ruining the place be her shame! It was after your man came nosing around about the trees that I put a lock on every gate. In fact, if it was he who had the cheek to remove the lock from the meadow gate, I have a spare one inside in the house that will guarantee that no man or dog will come back in here unknownst to me.'

'Maybe he's still in the grounds,' Joe said.

'No. He'll have doubled back the way he came once he saw me talking to the two of you.'

'But where were you while we were all chasing around?' Joe asked. 'If you didn't notice three of us and a big black dog, would you notice one man?'

Mr. Gallagher stared hard at Joe. He obviously didn't like the way Joe had spoken to him. Neither did Maeve. Joe had sounded almost like their father when he was feeling cross with the world.

Mr. Gallagher said, 'Since you want to know the details of my business, I'll tell you. I walked down as far as the main gates to see if there was a message for me. The phone here has been cut off, and so young Brian Costello that got my job as postman calls to my daughter before he sets out on his rounds. She'll give him a note to stick in the front gate or under a stone by the gate pillar if it's raining. Does that satisfy you?'

'I didn't mean to be rude,' Joe said hastily. 'I just wondered why you hadn't noticed what was going on. That's all.'

'And I should have more sense than to take offence,' Mr. Gallagher said, 'for I know you mean well. But you can rest assured that I'll make quite sure that the house and all the gates are well and truly secure before I go off to the Macra na Feirme outing beyond in Slane this afternoon. Are you sure you wouldn't like to come too? My daughter will be collecting me at the front gate.'

'No, no thanks,' Joe said. 'We'll go back out through the meadow gate and find our way to the canal from there.'

'Righto,' Mr. Gallagher said. 'I'll fetch the lock and follow you in a few minutes.'

The old man went back into the house. Suddenly the same unnerving silence, the same feeling of being lost in time descended on the parkland. 'I don't like this at all,' Joe said. 'I don't believe timber merchants go around knocking on people's doors, trying to buy trees.'

'Maybe he was like the people who tried to buy the oil lamps from Miss Grogan last year. They said they were antique dealers but they were really people who bought things and put them into auctions. Maybe there are people who go around finding out if there are trees for sale and then get a commission if the deal goes through.'

'I still don't like it,' Joe said. 'What about the look on the man's face when he got up out of the ditch?'

'Maybe he felt stupid about being caught hiding in the ditch. I know I would.'

'But why was he hiding there?'

'If Mr. Gallagher isn't worried about it, why should we be? You know how grown-ups can be if they think you are interfering.'

'That man took the lock off the meadow gate. That's worse than interfering.'

'Mr. Gallagher could well have forgotten to put it back on after visiting the Breens. He's always forgetting things. He left the bag of letters outside Miss Grogan's one day and couldn't remember what he'd done with them. Now let's get out of here. I'll race you as far as the canal bank.'

'It's too hot for racing,' Joe said but Maeve was already headed for the gate. Joe had no option but to follow.

He glanced back when he arrived at the gate. Mr. Gallagher was coming down the front steps. The sun glistened on the lock and the length of chain in his hand. Somehow they didn't seem like enough to keep intruders out of the parkland.

4 The Black Dog Again

The meadow stretched out under Maeve's feet like a great green cloak. Her relief at being out of the parkland was so enormous that she plunged straight through the hedge into the next field before she thought to make sure that Joe was following her.

He was, but very slowly, hardly running at all. Then he stopped altogether to watch Mr. Gallagher put the lock and chain on the meadow gate.

The old man waved to them and suddenly Maeve had an image of the house at dead of night, with empty room after empty room, the white sheets on the furniture and Mr. Wiltshaw staring sternly down from his portrait, while Mr. Gallagher slept in that narrow bed in that tiny attic, right up under the roof.

Maeve's new-found feeling of relief vanished. Once again, she was worried and uncertain.

Joe's first words, when he caught up with her, showed that he shared her uneasiness. 'I'm not the least bit happy about that man we saw in the parkland. I think we should have a word with him. He can't have got far with that limp, and if he's making for the road he'll have to use the path along the canal.'

Any other time to hear Joe sound as though he was imitating their father would have made Maeve giggle but there was nothing amusing about the present situation.

They quickly crossed the last of the fields and reached

the canal. They had a clear view along the path in both directions and there was no sign of the man.

'He could have cut across the Breens' land,' Maeve said, 'and ended up on the road to Sallins.'

'No, this is the natural way for him to come. There'd be too much risk of him being seen by one of the Breens and asked to explain himself.'

Then they heard the dog bark but the sound came from the opposite side of the canal. And then there was the dog himself appearing, as if by magic, through a growth of blackthorn. He spotted the children and without a moment's hesitation jumped into the canal and swam over to them, looking more like a seal than a dog with his black head shining above the water. He shook himself several times, sending a spray of water over Joe and Maeve.

Then he began the half-dance, half-bounce routine that he seemed to reserve for greeting humans. Wet coat or no wet coat, Maeve could not resist hugging him. 'I'm half-inclined to call him "Ghost" because of the way he keeps vanishing and reappearing.'

'You can't call a dog Ghost. He should have a sensible name like Darkie.' The dog gave a delighted bark. 'Hey! I think I got it right. "Darkie"! Is that your name? Is it?'

Darkie tried to lick Joe's face as he had tried with the man in the ditch.

Maeve said, 'Maybe the man who was hiding in the ditch was trying to get rid of the dog. People do drive out into the country and dump their unwanted pets.' But even as she spoke, Maeve knew that she was just trying to find an easy explanation for what had been happening.

'He wants us to follow him again. I'm sure of it. He has something – or someone – he wants us to see.'

'Well it can hardly be the man,' Maeve said. 'He would never have got to the other side of the canal so quickly, unless, of course, he did like Darkie has just done and swam across.' She looked down into the still water. 'It's too deep to paddle.'

'We'll use the bridge,' Joe said, 'where the tip-head was.'

The path along the canal bank, first made for the horses and men that had dragged the barges to the great waterway junction at Robertstown, was pitted with holes and breaks that, even on so warm a day, were soft and slippy and likely to send a careless runner into the thick mud that lined the bank. But the children kept well away from the edge and soon the bridge that, from a distance, looked like a giant pencil-stroke, came into firmer shape.

The dog ran alongside them for a few seconds and then, as if losing patience with such a long way round, plunged once again into the water.

'I hope he waits for us,' Joe panted.

'So do I,' Maeve said, and then putting on an extra burst of speed she reached the bridge well ahead of Joe.

The tip-head on the other side had been closed and wired off but, still, huge flocks of scavenging seagulls screamed overhead as if in fury at having been deprived by the County Council's bulldozers of access to the rotting garbage.

The smell from the tip-head was very noticeable and Maeve and Joe automatically wrinkled their noses.

Darkie, his tail wagging more furiously than ever,

waited for them to get within reach of him and, at once, went back through the barrier of blackthorn. 'I'll be in bits by the time all this is over,' Joe declared. 'I've torn my tee-shirt once already this morning.'

'Never mind,' Maeve said. 'I'll sew it for you later on.'

Maeve mend his tee-shirt? The last time she had sewn anything for him, it had taken their mother two hours to unpick the resulting tangled knot. But this was not the moment to discuss that sort of thing for Darkie was leading them along the perimeter fence of the tip-head and Joe was almost asphyxiated by the pong.

But Maeve seemed quite unaffected or else, like Joe, thought it better not to inhale more than she had to of the stink.

The tip-head fence swung to the right, cutting across a raised area of ground, like a small hill that had been cut in half. A huge piece of ancient machinery lay on its side as though it had collapsed under the weight of its own rust.

'There must have been a sand quarry here at one time. The tip-head must have been started on the rest of it,' Maeve said.

'And look at that!' Joe pointed at the recently-crushed fume-stained grass close to the quarry. 'There was a car or a van here recently. It's a perfect hiding-place with the remains of a road for an easy get-away.'

The remains of the road that had served the quarry were clearly visible, leading to an opening on to the back road to Robertstown.

'Only whose van could it have been? Here, Darkie! Where are you off to now?'

The dog who had been nosing around in the sand was on the move again, this time following the tyre tracks.

'You can't catch up with a car or a van no matter how fast you run and if a farmer sees a strange dog on the loose, he might think you were after his sheep. Come back here now!' Joe grabbed Darkie by the collar and began to drag him towards the wire-fence of the tip-head. But suddenly with a great twist, Darkie freed himself from Joe's grip.

The strength behind the move was such that Joe was thrown completely off balance and fell back against Maeve.

For what seemed like an eternity they stood in space, and then crashed with such force into the tip-head wire that the supporting struts gave under their combined weight and they descended into what, to Joe, was like a whirlpool of dust and rubble and, worst of all, a smell more sickening than anything that had been wafted from the tip-head previously.

Then, through the confusion of dust, rubbish and smell, Joe heard the sound of a motor bike fading quickly into the distance along the canal road.

'Get up off me, you great lump!' Maeve pushed angrily at her brother who was half-lying, half-sitting on top of her. 'Talk about me falling off walls, when you don't seem to stay on your feet at all when anything happens.'

'The dog is gone and there was a motor cycle just now on the canal road, going, I think, towards Naas.'

'Lots of motor cycles use the canal road.'

'This one was different. It just seemed to come out of nowhere.'

'Like the dog, do you mean?'

'Yes, I think that's exactly what I mean.' He glanced at the marks on the grass again but they had definitely been made by a four-wheel vehicle.

Maeve was gazing at her clothes in horror. 'Well we can't do anything in this state. And I seem to have lost my picnic. What was left of it.'

'I've lost mine too.'

'We'll have to go home and change. I only hope Miss Grogan doesn't see us or smell us.'

They pushed quickly through the blackthorn out on to the canal road. There was no need or no point in taking care of their clothes now. They were surely only good for burning. 'Well at least we won't have to mend that silly tee-shirt of yours,' Maeve said.

But Joe wasn't listening. He was gazing at the remains

of a broken-down cottage just visible behind what once must have been a garden wall and hedge.

The soft ground that had not yet been baked by the sun was, like the grass in the quarry, criss-crossed with tyre marks but here they were unmistakably of the kind made by a motor cycle.

'No wonder we didn't hear it until the very last second,' Joe said. 'The motor bike was parked in the cottage. We were being watched every step of the way and then, when it suited whoever owns the bike, a signal was given to Darkie that he would be sure to respond to.'

'You mean Darkie's gone off on the pillion seat of a motor bike?'

'Or sitting on the front between the rider and the handlebars. I've seen that on the TV.'

'But this isn't the TV.' Then she sighed and said, 'Which makes it all the worse. I only hope no one at all sees us like this, never mind just Miss Grogan.'

'I don't see how we can make certain of that unless of course ...'

'Unless of course nothing!' Maeve grinned, knowing at once what Joe had in mind. The quickest way home was by way of the meadow. The quickest way back to the meadow was to follow Darkie's example.

Five strokes brought them to the opposite bank. The degree of total immersion lessened the terrible odour from their clothes momentarily, but only momentarily, for then the heat of the sun on the damp material suddenly made the smell stronger than ever.

'Let's go faster,' Maeve said.

Within minutes, they were back at the meadow gate into the Wiltshaw estate. The parkland looked completely deserted, the house even more like a great stone creature lost in time.

The children had no urge to speak, as once more the strange, oppressive mood of the place came over them. Silently they followed the wall back to the weed-clogged lane, pausing only when they reached the barrier of cow parsley to listen for the sound of traffic on the road.

At the outskirts of Innisdara, they dodged down the back street, past a row of buildings, once livery stables, but now used as stores by Mr. Ryan of the shop and Mr. Kelly of the pub. The gate into the Maguires' garden was next to the last of these buildings. The children opened the back door of their house.

'Another empty house,' Joe said. 'It's a morning for empty houses.'

'And lost picnics and falls,' Maeve added. 'To say nothing of strange men and stray dogs!'

'What are we going to do with our clothes?'

'Dump them in a bag in the garden shed.' Maeve pulled off her shoes and socks and left them on the mat. 'We'll explain what happened when Mam gets home.'

She ran upstairs and into her bedroom. It was golden with sunlight and as warm as if heated by a huge fire. She wished she could open a window to let some air in, but Miss Grogan might spot her and come across to discover why they had sneaked home down the back street.

What would Miss Grogan say if they told her what had happened? Would she think they had made it up just as an excuse for ruining their clothes? Would anyone, in fact, believe that it might have been due to something more sinister than an accident or carelessness on their part?

5 An Old Photograph

Maeve turned away from the window and saw herself in the looking-glass of the wardrobe. She really was a terrible sight, and if her clothes smelt then so did she. She removed her jeans and tee-shirt and put on her dressing gown. 'I'm going to have a bath,' she called out to Joe. 'You'd better have one as well.'

'What? In the middle of the morning?' Joe looked out of his room. He had already put on clean clothes, but instead of looking better he looked worse, with his filthy face and plastered-down hair sticking out of the neck of a different tee-shirt.

'It'll only take a few minutes and it'll give us time to think. I'll call you when I've finished. You can bring these things down with your own.' She handed Joe her jeans and tee-shirt and went into the bathroom.

When Joe opened the back door, he realized that the garden, which had seemed so quiet a few minutes back, was, in fact, heavy with the sound of bees. Two butterflies hovered around the vegetable patch. Joe hadn't noticed any of this a few seconds before even though butterflies were becoming so rare a sight. 'Time to think,' Maeve had said, and she was right. They had been rushing around the countryside, tripping and falling and jumping not only into the canal but also to the conclusion that there was actually something sinister going on.

Inside the shed, there were several plastic bags under

a box of newspapers. His father often kept newspapers if there was something in them that interested him, and when Mrs. Maguire insisted that he clear them out of his study he still hated to throw them away. So they would be stored in the shed until they disintegrated and were barely useful for starting a bonfire.

Joe lifted the box up off the bags and then gaped in amazement at the newspaper on the top of the pile. There, staring almost challengingly at him, was a picture of a man with deep-set staring eyes. Next to the man was a woman, trying to smile, but the smile had become a squint as though she was staring into bright sunshine. In her arms she was holding a black labrador pup.

Joe sat down and opened the newspaper more fully. But the newspaper had been folded across the names of the people and the time in the garden shed had caused the print to brown and fade so that the words could no longer be read.

'What are you doing?' Maeve's voice made him jump. 'I've been calling you to tell you that I'm finished in the bathroom.'

'Look what I found! Could be the man in the ditch!

Maeve examined the picture sceptically. 'That's a bit far-fetched ... yet that young dog could be Darkie. What date is the newspaper?'

Joe looked at the top of the sheet. He could just make out the words — *The Leinster Leader*, 7 June, 1977. It was now June 1985. Their father had held on to the newspaper for eight years and left it open at the photograph, which surely meant that the photograph was the reason he kept it in the first place. 'If only we could make out the names.'

'That's no problem.' Maeve straightened up. 'We know what date the picture appeared. Newspapers keep back issues. All we have to do is to telephone *The Leinster Leader* office in Naas and ask them if we can have a look at the files.'

'But how do we get to Naas?'

'Hitch a lift. That'll be easy once we get out on the road to Prosperous. Go and have your bath and I'll see what there is to eat after I've put this stuff away.'

Maeve folded the faded newspaper carefully and put it on top of the others in the box. As she bundled the clothes into a plastic bag, the Angelus began to sound out over the countryside. Could Darkie and the man hear it as well? She closed the shed door firmly. She had no time to waste daydreaming.

There were eggs in the fridge and beans in the cupboard; those with some toast would do fine.

As soon as she'd set the table, she telephoned *The Leinster Leader*. The woman she spoke to at first seemed doubtful about Joe and Maeve being able to look at eight-year-old copies of the paper at such short notice.

'Oh please,' Maeve pleaded.

'Well, I'll see what I can do.'

The food was ready by the time Joe came downstairs. Usually he only looked that clean on Sunday mornings.

'I've been thinking, like you suggested,' he said, as soon as he had swallowed a mouthful of beans. 'We'd better be careful that we don't end up in the wrong.'

'It'll be easier when we know the man's name. I've telephoned the paper and I think we'll be let see the issue with that picture in it.'

Joe nodded. Then he said, 'Are you afraid?'

'Yes, a bit but then I'd be stupid not to be.'

'Do you want to wait until Dad and Mam get back from Dublin?'

'No. It might be important that we find out what we can before that.'

'Right.' Joe put the plates and the pot and pan to soak in the sink. 'They can wait until later.'

The town dozed in the high noon sun as Joe and Maeve slipped down the back street to where a grass triangle marked the road to Prosperous. They stood and waited. Then Maeve lay on the grass. 'I can feel the sun burning my face.' She glanced up at the sky. It was the colour of faded denim with no sign of a cloud. The air was absolutely still. The trees and hedges drooped like weary soldiers on guard duty.

A small dust storm rattled around the bend towards them. It was the Brady brothers' van driven by Dave, the youngest. He slowed down and stopped when the children waved at him. 'How are you? What's on?'

'We need a lift into Naas,' Joe said.

'Nothing easier,' Dave said. 'That's where I'm headed myself. Hop in the back.'

Maeve and Joe squatted down on a pile of dusty sacks. 'We'll be as dirty in a few minutes as if we hadn't changed our clothes at all,' Maeve thought crossly. But really she was cross because Dave hadn't invited her to sit in the front seat. Maeve admired Dave greatly.

'Are you on holidays now?'

'It's the first day,' Joe said.

'Lucky you.'

39

'I thought you couldn't wait to leave school,' Maeve said, 'to help your brothers build houses.'

Dave grinned. 'Oh that's true enough all right. But it doesn't mean that I don't miss the long summer break. Do you know what I'd do if I had a couple of months off? I'd get a motor bike and go off to America and drive for hundreds and hundreds of miles along those State highways. In fact only this morning I saw a fellow on a motor bike ...'

'What sort of fellow? Did you know him?' Joe leaned forward so that he might more easily hear Dave's answer above the rattle of the engine.

'Never saw him before in my entire life but sure, since they finished that new bit of the motorway, you get all kinds of people coming this way to have a look at the canals and the bog.'

'Did he have a black dog with him?'

'On a motor bike? Are you mad?' Dave pulled into the side and turned the engine off. 'What's going on?'

Maeve and Joe looked at each other. 'We'd better tell him,' Maeve said. So they did.

When they had finished, Dave said, 'It sounds odd all right. Very odd indeed.' He stared thoughtfully out the window. 'It's a bit hard to know what to do for the best. If only everyone wasn't off at the Macra na Feirme outing. The place is like a Clint Eastwood Western, not a thing moving in the sunbaked landscape except with the Man-with-no-Name.' Dave was a great admirer of Clint Eastwood.

'Except that Clint Eastwood is usually the good guy,' Joe said.

'Not always,' Dave said, 'but then you can't judge a

person by the way he looks.'

'And once we get to Naas, we may soon have a name for him,' Maeve said. 'It's what we do then that's the problem.'

'Wait for your father to come back from Dublin. After all, he's the official representative of Julia Wiltshaw around here. I'll keep an eye out for a motor bike and a black dog.'

Dave drove on, and from the way he changed gears gave the impression that he liked to imagine that the van was a horse and that he was riding the range.

The wide street of Prosperous narrowed at the steep-backed canal bridge. The children looked out the back window of the van but saw no black dogs and no motor bikes.

Under the dome of blue sky, the Naas by-pass was like something out of a futuristic film with the traffic, as though operated by remote control, crossing over and under the network of roads.

'I have to go to Chadwicks to collect some stuff they've ordered for the bungalow we're building,' Dave said. 'Wait for me outside *The Leinster Leader* office.'

Maeve and Joe brushed the dust of the sacks from their hair and clothes as they hurried past the Chinese restaurant and around the corner into the main street of the town. *The Leinster Leader* office was next to the Court House. The young woman in the front office took them into a small room with a table and two chairs. Then she brought in a volume of bound copies of the newspaper. 'You should find what you're looking for in here.'

The children carefully turned over the pages until they saw the date, 7 June, 1977. The photograph was much clearer than in the faded copy Mr. Maguire had stored in the garden shed. The words under the photograph read, 'Miss Julia Wiltshaw of Wiltshaw House, Innisdara, with her nine-month-old labrador, Darkie, who won first prize in his class at the Barretsbridge Dog Show. Also pictured is Mr. Francis Callaghan who showed Darkie for Miss Wiltshaw.'

'I told you that was the man who was in the ditch,' Joe said triumphantly. 'And he must be from around here. It all ties up!'

'But why didn't we recognize Julia Wiltshaw as soon as we saw the picture?'

'She looked quite different then, with the way her face is all screwed up and her hair so long! Anyway we've only ever seen her a few times,' Maeve said. 'But if Francis Callaghan knows Julia Wiltshaw so well, why is he sneaking around the estate? And why has he Julia's dog with him?'

The street outside was even warmer than when they had gone into the newspaper office. They stood in the shade of a chemist's shop awning, waiting for Dave. A trickle of cars moved along the main street.

Suddenly, Maeve said, 'Maybe we should look inside that cottage. Dave could drive back down along the canal. It would hardly be out of his way at all.'

The door of the chemist's shop swung open. The children moved to one side to allow the customer to pass and found themselves staring straight into Francis Callaghan's face. Francis did not give the slightest flicker of recognition. Then he turned the corner.

'I'm going after him. You wait here for Dave.' And before Maeve could stop him, Joe had set off in pursuit.

6 The Cottage by the Canal

Francis Callaghan was just a few yards ahead of Joe. His limp seemed worse than ever but he tried to move quickly, not once looking back to see if he was being followed. A sign, in black and white, over his head read 'Lounge Bar'. Francis, without slowing down, stepped in through the swing doors.

Joe ran forward. He knew he was not allowed by law to go into a pub without a good excuse. A drink of water? It sounded feeble but the day was so warm it might just do.

The inside of the pub was as dark as a cave after the bright sunlight and empty except for the barman polishing glasses. 'Do you want something?' he asked crossly, 'or are you just passing through as well?'

'Passing through?'

'Like that fellow a second ago; in one door and out the other.' The barman pointed at a second pair of swing doors that led back out on to the main street.

Maeve was running by as Joe stepped out on to the pavement. 'There he is,' she said, pointing at the back of the limping man. 'I saw him come out of the pub.'

As if he had heard Maeve's voice, Francis looked back at the children. Then, suddenly he stepped into the roadway. A car screeched to a stop, almost knocking down a cyclist. The people on the pavement hurried forward to see that no one had been hurt. Maeve and Joe were encircled by the crowd, and by the time they emerged, Francis Callaghan was nowhere to be seen.

'Maybe he went back to the pub.' Joe looked towards it and saw Dave getting out of the van in front of *The Leinster Leader* office. 'Dave can look for him in there.'

'But where are you off to?'

'Down towards Lawlor's Hotel and the supermarkets. The motor bike may be parked there.'

'But you'll be careful.'

'Of course I'll be careful.' He grinned. 'This is better than looking for Finn's Way! I might get the number on the motor bike. If Francis Callaghan is not in the pub, ask Dave to meet me outside the cinema.'

People turned and stared as Joe ran along the pavement. Mothers snatched children out of his path. Dogs tried to decide whether to follow him or bark at him, but Joe was unaware of the disturbance he was causing.

In the carpark at Superquinn, there were at least six motor bikes. There were even more in front of Lawlor's Hotel and yet more around Quinnsworth. Joe had set himself a hopeless task. He had no way of identifying Francis Callaghan's from so many machines.

He went back to the cinema. The van, with Maeve in the front passenger seat, was waiting. 'It's no good,' Joe said as he climbed in on the sacks. 'I couldn't find him.'

'Dave says he's heard his brothers mention a Francis Callaghan whose father used to be a vet around here. But he has no idea where he lives now,' Maeve said.

'A vet's son?'

'Yes,' said Maeve, 'and Dave is going to take us to have a look at the old cottage.'

'But only on condition that you don't do anything stupid,' Dave warned. He drove back down the main

44

street and turned right down the side of the Town Hall. The section of canal that ran parallel to the main street had been cleared and restored by the local people, many of whom sat on the wooden seats, talking and keeping an eye on the children playing along the banks.

'It's like a huge garden,' Maeve thought and wished she knew more of the history of the canal. She wasn't even sure if it was the Royal Canal or the Grand Canal. She vowed that as soon as they'd solved the mystery of the black dog and Francis Callaghan, her next project would be to learn all about Irish canals. 'But what about Finn's Way?' a nagging little voice in her head reminded her.

The van passed a flour mill and soon had left the town houses behind. The flat countryside stretched out again on all sides. Maeve could see the ribbons of seagulls circling and wheeling around the closed tip-head. Dave stopped the van in front of the derelict cottage.

All three of them got out and picked their way through the wild-grown hedge. The cottage was in a very bad state. One section of the roof had fallen in, filling the interior with its rubble. Dave cast an expert eye around the place. He pointed at a sheet of corrugated iron in what must have been the kitchen. 'That's not part of the original building. Someone brought that in specially.'

He lifted the corrugated sheet and underneath it was a sleeping-bag with a protective plastic cover.

Under the remains of a collapsed kitchen table, there was another plastic-wrapped bundle, with a biscuit tin containing a bottle of orange and two packets of biscuits inside.

Dave pointed to where the back door had been. Outside there was a hollow filled with the dry leaves of last autumn. The leaves had been flattened as if by a weight. 'If Francis Callaghan knows this cottage, that could be where he keeps his motor bike and probably sleeps as well. It'd be as comfortable as any bed. It's an ideal set-up for him as well if he wants to get to Wiltshaw House. You can see the top of the trees around the house from here. And none of these things would rouse any suspicion. Supposing the guards came and questioned Francis. He could claim to be a fisherman out from Dublin who just decided to stay in an old ruin overnight.'

'But I still don't understand how he got back here so quickly from Wiltshaw House with his sore foot. Could there be another way out of the estate?' Joe asked.

'A secret way that no one except himself and Julia Wiltshaw know about?' Maeve's question caused a great silence.

'But the place belongs to Julia Wiltshaw.' It was Dave who broke the silence. 'We keep forgetting that. If Francis Callaghan is a friend of hers, why would he be behaving like a criminal, like someone with something to hide?'

'Whatever he's up to, he's bound to come back here,' Joe said. 'He knows that we can identify him but he may not know that we've found his hiding-place. Well I'm good at hiding too.'

'What are you getting at?' Dave asked quickly.

'We need to get the number of the motor bike,' Joe explained. 'Dad will need to know that if he has to make enquiries. The only other evidence that Francis was around the place is the sleeping-bag and the box of food. I'll bet he'll come back to take those away and to put whatever he bought in the chemist on his sore ankle!'

'I only agreed to stop here on condition you and Maeve did nothing foolish,' Dave said quickly.

'But it's not foolish,' Joe said. 'It's the only sensible thing to do. He won't come near the place at all if he sees your van outside, so the sooner you move it the better.'

47

A few yards away from the cottage, in the direction of the tip-head, three barrels had been left after the tip had been closed. 'I can hide behind those and keep watch,' Joe said. 'Maeve, you go back to Innisdara with Dave and see if Mam and Dad are back yet.'

'I'll drop the stuff in the van at the bungalow,' Dave said. 'Then I'll come back here. Joe can see the van a fair distance away down this road. If he wants me to stop, he can give a signal by standing up. If he doesn't want me to stop, he just stays out of sight. I'll drive around the bend and walk back through the fields.'

Maeve had to admit that Dave's plan was sensible. 'If Mam and Dad aren't back, I might even be able to find that letter that came this morning and telephone them in Dublin.'

'Only don't go frightening them,' Joe warned.

'As if I would,' Maeve replied indignantly.

Joe watched the van drive out of sight. Then he settled down behind the barrels. The sunlight danced off the canal. There was a line of delicate grasses and tall bullrushes just visible through a space between the barrels. Strange to think that the canal had once been like a motorway with barge after barge taking people and goods across Ireland.

Joe moved slightly back into the shade of the hedge. His eyes felt heavy and he realized that he was falling asleep. At once, he sat up straight. A horsefly buzzed around him. More flies became aware of him and joined in the exploration of his head. He swatted them but that seemed only to encourage them. Suddenly his mouth was dry with the taste of tinned beans. He thought of the bottle of orange in the biscuit box.

7 Francis Callaghan

Now that Dave had left her at the grass triangle, Maeve suddenly began to have doubts as to the wisdom of what they were doing. If her own parents weren't back, ought she confide in someone else? The second house on the left belonged to the Bradys. The Brady brothers had put so many extensions and additions on to it that it now looked like several different houses stuck together. Maeve stopped outside it.

'There's no one there.' Brian Costello, the postman, stopped and spoke to her. 'Mrs. Brady went off a few minutes ago with Brigid Gallagher and her father to the Macra na Feirme outing. I'll be going over myself as soon as I can. Do you want me to give the Bradys a message? Is there anything the matter?'

'No, not really.'

'Not really? That's not much of an answer. Where's Joe?'

'Oh, he's around somewhere.'

'You sound as though you've lost him!'

'No, he's all right.'

'I see.' Brian Costello stared so long and hard at Maeve that she was glad of the excuse of Mr. and Mrs. Ryan coming out of their shop to look away.

'There'll be no business done here this afternoon,' Mr. Ryan declared, 'so we thought we might as well go to the outing as well. Do you and Joe want a lift? It'll be a great bit of gas.'

'Oh no, thanks all the same, Mr. Ryan. We have to wait for Mam and Dad to get back.'

'You haven't seen Miss Grogan then?' Mrs. Ryan asked.

'Not since this morning.'

'She was looking for you. It seems she had a message for you from Dublin so you'd best go along now and ask her.'

'Yes, all right, I will.' Maeve managed to smile as she hurried off to Miss Grogan's house but the doubts in her mind were rapidly turning to a growing fear that things were going very wrong, and that she was not making a very good job of hiding it. Brian Costello seemed to be able to read her thoughts.

Miss Grogan opened the door at once. 'Oh, so there you are at long last. You got the note.' Seeing the blank look on Maeve's face, she continued, 'I called over to your house. You weren't there so I left a note. Your mother telephoned to say they'd be late back from Dublin, delayed by business, a problem over Julia Wiltshaw. You and Joe are to come and have your supper with me.' Miss Grogan waved at the Ryans as they drove by. 'Everyone seems to have gone off to that outing. I think there's only you and me and Joe left in Innisdara. By the way, where's Joe?'

'Oh he's not back yet.'

'Back from where?'

'The canal.'

'I hope he's not gone swimming by himself. That can be very dangerous.'

'No. He just wanted to have a look.'

Miss Grogan's eyes glinted behind her glasses. 'At

the canal? Has he not been looking at it all his life?'

'He found an old cottage near the tip-head.'

'And what is there to interest him in that old place?' Miss Grogan stared at Maeve again. 'You need some cream on your face. I have some grand stuff upstairs.'

Maeve followed Miss Grogan inside the house. The hall was so clean that it was hard to imagine that anyone ever did anything so ordinary as walk on it. The kitchen was as spotless as the hall. 'Wait here.'

As the calm coolness of the shining little house descended over Maeve, she wished she could ask Miss Grogan's advice. But if Miss Grogan even suspected that Joe was hiding behind those barrels to spy on someone, she would have hysterics. If only there was someone left in Innisdara apart from Miss Grogan!

'Are you all right?' Miss Grogan had come back into the kitchen without Maeve hearing her. 'Irish people have to be careful about the sun. You'd best sit down and let me put the cream on.'

The effect of the cream was instantly soothing.

'Did you ever hear of the Callaghans?' It wasn't the way Maeve had planned it, but even at the risk of rousing Miss Grogan's suspicions, she had to ask the question.

'The Callaghans? Do you mean the vet, God rest his soul, that lived over Straffan way? I would have thought you'd be far too young to remember them!'

'Dave Brady mentioned them.'

'I wonder what put the Callaghans in his mind.' Miss Grogan applied a bit more cream. 'Maybe the Macra na Feirme outing brought their name up for both Mr. Callaghan and his wife were greatly respected and admired, which made the disgrace that the son brought on the family all the worse.'

'What disgrace?'

'Young Francis Callaghan got into terrible trouble over at Wiltshaw House shortly after his father died. He was a marvel with dogs, a gift he got from the father, I suppose, and he used help Julia with her labradors. Then one day he attacked one of the estate workers with a spade handle. I've heard it said that if one of the Breens hadn't heard the commotion, it might have ended in a murder charge.'

'Murder!'

'Yes and all for to steal the man's weekly wage! Of course, it was hushed up out of respect for Mrs. Callaghan but, all the same, the family name was ruined. Even Mr. Gallagher used dread meeting Francis on the road in case he tried to steal the letters from him. Eventually Mrs. Callaghan sold up and moved away.'

'And has Francis never been back?'

'What would bring him back, unless some foolish notion of revenge? Maeve, where are you going?'

'I have to tell Joe something.'

'But you said he was out at that old cottage.' Miss Grogan put down the tin of cream. 'Is there something wrong? Now that I think of it, you're wearing different clothes than you were in this morning.'

But Maeve was out of the house and running down the street as though a couple of devils were chasing her.

The buzz of flies around Joe's head seemed to have grown louder and more determined and then there was what sounded like an electric saw. An electric saw?

Trees? Was someone cutting down the trees around Wiltshaw House? Joe clicked into an upright position and saw the sky through the tangle of the hedge. He had fallen asleep in spite of his determination not to! He also realized that the sounds he had heard through his sleep were neither of flies nor of saws but of a motor bike.

The roar of the engine reduced and stopped. Joe peered over the top of the barrels. A tall figure, wearing a crash helmet, was wheeling a motor bike through the hedge and into the cottage.

Joe dropped down into the ditch and moved under the line of blackthorns, grateful that the dark-coloured tee-shirt that he had changed into would give him some degree of camouflage among the shadows and leaf patterns.

The tall figure came out the other side of the cottage and walked across the leafy hollow into the adjoining field. This was the chance Joe needed to get the licence number of the motor bike. Keeping his head down, he reached the chimney-breast of the cottage. The motor bike was parked around the front, its licence plates covered with dust.

He rubbed quickly at the rear plate but, even as the numbers and letters became visible, the figure with the crash helmet came back into the cottage. He wore a check shirt and jeans and carried a canvas-wrapped bundle. He took off his crash helmet and placed it and the bundle down beside him before reaching for the biscuit tin under the corrugated metal. Then, sensing that he was being watched, he spun around and, for the first time, Joe could see the man's face clearly. It was Brian Costello, the postman!

'Brian! What are you …?'

Joe never got to finish the question for there was a sudden loud sound of barking from the road behind him. Brian ran quickly out of the cottage. 'Come here, you brute! Come here!'

Darkie was standing by the canal, his coat shining with water from yet another swim. He wagged his tail at Brian but made no attempt to move closer. 'Come here!' Brian repeated the command. Darkie stood his ground.

'He doesn't trust you,' Joe said.

'Let's see how you get on then!'

Joe held a hand out. 'Here, Darkie!'

Darkie moved a few inches in the direction of Joe. Joe clicked his fingers. 'Good dog, Darkie! Good dog!' The dog moved close enough for Joe to pat his head.

'How do you know his name?'

'It's what I would call a dog this colour.' Joe glanced up and down the road. There was no sign of a car or a bicycle or even a pedestrian. And how he wished there was! He had to do something, to say something to improve the atmosphere. 'I didn't know you had a motor bike.'

'It belongs to a friend. Have you and the dog met before?'

'I saw him around the place this morning. Maeve and I thought he might be a stray.'

'Stray dogs can be dangerous or lead people into danger. You'd be better off going to the outing. Is that your sister?'

Maeve had just reached the tip-head, her arms waving like windmills.

'It might be as well if you both took my advice, for it's

good advice.' Brian put the bundle on the back of the motor bike, kick-started the machine and zoomed off back in the direction of Naas with Darkie doing his best to keep up with him.

By the time Maeve drew level with Joe, dog and machine had reached the bend in the road. 'Was that Brian Costello?' Maeve struggled for breath. 'I ran all the way out here in case it was Francis Callaghan. Miss Grogan said he tried to murder someone once!'

'Maybe that's why Brian tried to warn me off!'

'I saw Brian in Innisdara just a short while ago. He asked me where you were.'

'And came rushing back here in case I found a bundle that was hidden outside in the hollow.'

'But where did he get the motor bike from?'

'I wish I knew. I'm parched. I'm going to have a drink of that orange.'

'Do you think you should?' Maeve asked. 'How do we know it's just orange?'

Joe reluctantly agreed that what Maeve said was true but all the same the idea of a long cool drink was really getting to him. He gave the stone at his feet a frustrated little kick and had hardly completed the move when there, suspended in the branches of the hedge, was the canvas bundle Brian Costello had come back for.

'It must have fallen off the back of the motor bike when he sped off like that.'

Quickly he unwrapped the canvas. Inside there was a chain cutter, a pliers and a jemmy. 'These must have been used to cut the chain on the meadow gate.'

'But why hide them here?'

'So that Brian could collect them.'

'But collect them for who?' Maeve had a sudden thought, so sensible that she knew it must be right.

She walked through the ruined cottage, across the leaf-filled hollow and into the next field. The deserted quarry was clearly visible as indeed any vehicle waiting there would be.

The cottage was the ideal place to meet or to signal from or, perhaps more important, to make sure it was safe to go to Wiltshaw House across the meadow.

'Whoever was waiting in the quarry could have left those tools for Brian Costello. Maybe it's a good place to call Darkie from too. He couldn't have kept up with the motor bike for very long. Let's try whistling.'

There was no response to their whistling. Maeve cupped her hands around her mouth and yelled, 'Darkie! Darkie!'

'He can't be so far away that he can't hear that.'

'Where did he come from just now?'

'Swam across the canal by the look of him.'

'Then maybe he's gone back that way to Wiltshaw House when he couldn't keep up with the motor bike. There is a connection between Francis Callaghan and the estate. Francis, according to Miss Grogan, may have come back looking for revenge.'

'What do we do now?'

'In fact,' said Maeve, 'we should go back out on the road and wait for Dave. I just hope we won't be too late to help maybe Darkie and whoever else is in trouble.'

8 Intruders!

'I can't believe that Brian Costello is mixed up in anything crooked,' Dave said. The trees of the Wiltshaw estate were visible now over the top of the parkland wall. 'And yet someone must be. Those certainly look like break-in tools that you found.' He stopped the van at the mouth of the lane. 'Wait here for me. I'll park outside my house and come straight back on foot.'

The children stepped inside the coolness of the lane. More than ever, it seemed like a dark green tunnel removed from the real world.

'Should we see if the door in the wall is still locked?' Joe asked.

'Better not until Dave gets back. He'll know what to do.' Then she blushed in case Joe might guess how much she admired Dave but Joe was staring in the direction of the parkland wall as though he had suddenly developed x-ray vision. 'I'm just thinking,' he said. 'Brian Costello and Francis Callaghan and Julie Wiltshaw are all more or less the same age. They must have all known each other. Mr. Gallagher told us that Brian Costello brings messages from the town to him. Brian would know when Mr. Gallagher was going to be away from the house.'

Once more silence descended until Dave arrived back, pushing through the cow parsley. 'Come on now. We'd better be both quick and quiet.' He tried the door. It was still locked.

'I got in over the wall,' Maeve said.

'Fell in is more like it,' Joe said.

Maeve ignored what she regarded as a totally un-
necessary remark. 'There's a pile of grass on the other
side that we can land on.'

'Fine! It's probably the quickest way.' Dave was tall
enough to reach the top of the wall with one jump. He
leaned down and helped Joe and Maeve up beside him.
They had a marvellous view of the parkland with the
front of the house and the part of the drive where Joe
had first seen Francis.

'It's like a painting,' Dave said.

'A painting you can jump into.' Joe jumped into the
pile of grass as he spoke. Dave laughed and followed.
Then Maeve. The grass sent up a cloud of seed and dust,
making all three of them sneeze. 'Better to get that over
with now than to have it happen later on,' Maeve said
pointedly to Joe as a way of paying him back for his remark about her falling off the wall.

But her sarcasm was wasted. Joe and Dave were
already moving off among the trees towards the house.
Maeve caught up with them. 'We'll have plenty of
cover, if we're careful,' Dave said, 'although the place
seems deserted.'

No sooner had he spoken than Francis Callaghan
came out of the front door, looked down the drive,
glanced at his watch and went back inside.

'He's waiting for someone and whoever it is, is late,'
Dave whispered.

'Look!' Maeve suddenly pointed at the drawing-room
windows. The shutters were being opened but the
bounce of light off the glass made it impossible to see

anything other than the outline of a figure.

'We're going to have to take a chance that Francis and whoever else might be with him are in the front of the house. We'll have to go in the back way. When I give the nod, we move as quickly as we can to the last of the trees and into the yard.'

The line of trees ended about four hundred yards from the side of the house. Dave gave a quick nod and they dashed across the open space into the yard and stood pressed against the back wall of the stables.

They waited a few seconds. Then Dave gave another nod and they ran across the cobbled yard.

At the back door, they paused once more and listened. No sound came from inside the house. Dave pushed the back door. It opened into the narrow, dim passage that led into the great flagged kitchen.

'We'll use the back stairs you told me about.' Dave's words were spoken so softly that his lips barely moved.

Maeve and Joe nodded and went through the archway to the foot of the narrow stairs. It was Joe's turn to whisper, 'I can't remember whether they creak or not.'

'The main thing is to be in a part of the house that no one can trap us in. We can listen and, maybe, see what's going on. We may even be able to sneak down the main staircase later on.'

Up through the house the three of them went, hearing only their own breathing and the slight sigh of the steps beneath their feet. On the top landing they paused, feeling as though they had accomplished their mission when in fact they knew it had only really started.

'There's something happening in the yard.' Dave stood well back from the window. Below him, he could see a large black van. Two men got out but he could see only the top of their heads as they entered the house.

Dave paused as if anxious to make his thoughts clear without revealing how worried he now was. 'There are two more men in the house now. The situation could be serious. We are going to have to do what maybe we ought to have done in the first place. Get help!'

'But there's only Miss Grogan left in Innisdara,' Maeve reminded him.

'She has a telephone. She can call the guards in Naas. But for the moment we'll have to wait a while. Which is Mr. Gallagher's room?'

'In here,' Maeve led the way, pushing as gently as possible on the door. It yielded easily to her touch and revealed, as it opened, Francis Callaghan trying to rise to his feet from where he had been sitting on the edge of the bed. His eyes were wide with the same expression as when the children had first seen him out in the parkland and Joe and Maeve both realized that Francis, far from being malevolent towards them, was in fact terrified at being seen once more.

'It's you again,' he said. 'Why do you keep interfering?' He looked at Dave. 'Who's this?'

'Dave Brady. He's come to help.'

'The only way any of you can help is to clear off. You are only making things worse.' The intensity of his words was made all the greater by the fact that he spoke them in a quick, hissing whisper. Then a great grimace of pain crossed his face and he half-sat, half-collapsed back on to the bed.

'We won't leave until we know what's going on.' Dave closed the door, obliging the three of them to enclose

Francis in a tight, determined semi-circle. 'Who are those men downstairs?'

'I can't tell you but they'll be coming looking for me soon. If they find you here ...'

'They'll what? They'll do what? Come on now, Francis Callaghan ...'

'How do you know my name?'

'We found out. That's all that matters. What will happen when those men come looking for you?'

'To me, probably, nothing ...'

'Then to who?' Dave looked as though he might decide to shake the information out of Francis.

'Is it the dog?' Maeve asked quickly. 'Might they harm Darkie?'

Francis managed a slight smile. 'So you know the dog's name as well.'

'Yes and about Brian Costello and the tools hidden in the cottage. But if it's not the dog, and Brian seems to be all right, who are you worried about?' Dave asked.

'Julia Wiltshaw!' The name just popped into Maeve's head. 'Miss Grogan said that the message from Dublin was that my parents would be back late because of a problem over Julia Wiltshaw. Are you worried about her?'

'I can't tell you. Just go away.'

'How can we do that without being seen by those men downstairs?' Joe asked the questions as calmly as if he was asking Francis to pass the butter, please. 'Is Julia in some kind of trouble? You'd better tell us.'

Francis closed his eyes and then, as if deciding there was no other solution to the problem, said 'Yes, she is'.

'How many more of them are there in the gang?'

'More?' Francis was amazed by the question.

'Are there just two?' Joe asked, sticking his thumbs in his belt and looking even more as though he was imitating his father. 'Because if there are only two, what I was thinking of was that Maeve here is a terrific runner. If we distract the men's attention by going down the front stairs, she could slip out the back and get help.'

'You could be putting Julia's life at risk. There are only two on the job here, as far as I know, but there have to be others involved. And I don't know where they've taken Julia. I've been trying to find out all morning.'

'With Darkie's help?'

'Poor Darkie is distracted, not knowing what's going on.'

'We're wasting time,' Dave said. 'Joe's plan is a good one. Maeve can phone the guards from Miss Grogan's.'

'No!' Francis said. He tried to rise again but the pain of his injured foot prevented him.

'You're in no position or condition to either agree or disagree.' Dave opened the door of the room. 'Off you go, Maeve. Count to ten before you go down the back stairs. Then, as fast as you can, back to Innisdara. The main gates are probably still unlocked after the van drove through.'

'No!' Francis made to grab at Maeve, but Joe jumped between them.

Maeve went to the top of the stairs and waited until Dave opened the door that led out on to the main corridor. Then, very slowly, she counted to ten and had just finished when Francis came lurching out of the tiny bedroom. Maeve at once started down the back staircase. In the other part of the house, she could hear a sudden sound of shouting and then a great confusion as though people were rushing around.

She reached the kitchen and tried to get some idea of what was going on. She suddenly very clearly heard Francis shout, 'There's a girl getting out the back way.'

Maeve sped to the back door and tugged at it. It wouldn't open. She looked desperately for a key in the lock but there was none. She tried to find a bolt but there didn't seem to be a bolt either. Then she saw one at the very top of the door, well out of her reach. If she stayed where she was, all hope of escape was cut off. She sped back across the kitchen and into the dining-room, almost tripping over a rolled-up rug that she was certain hadn't been there earlier in the day.

The sheet-covered table was the only possible hiding place. She flung herself under it just as a man came in from the hall. All she could see of him were his feet as he passed through into the kitchen. He came back almost at once, and spoke to the other man in the hall. 'She didn't get out the back door. She must be still upstairs. You keep those three covered. I'll use the back stairs. We'll soon flush her out.'

The feet passed across the dining-room and once more into the kitchen. Maeve counted to ten again and came out from under the table. She could see nothing of what was happening in the hall but the word 'covered' surely meant that the other man had a gun. The first man was charging upstairs, not caring how much noise he made, confident that she could not now get out of the house.

A row of kitchen chairs stood next to the dresser. Maeve easily lifted one and carried it to the back door. She tugged at the bolt and, within seconds, was out in the yard and headed for the protection of the trees.

9 Francis Explains

Joe and Dave did not dare take their eyes off the man in the hall below. He had a stocking mask over his face and in his hands a sawn-off shotgun.

Francis Callaghan stood half-propped against the bannister, trying to take some of the weight off his foot. For a moment, it seemed that the pain would once more prove too much for him, but when he tried to change his stance the man motioned with the shotgun. 'Not a muscle, not an inch, Francis Callaghan, or you and your friends will get it.'

'I didn't know they were in the house,' Francis insisted.

'Oh, sure.'

'I warned you about the girl, didn't I?' Francis said.

'Yeh, but where is she, if you were so anxious to prevent her leaving?'

The man who had been searching the bedrooms came to the top of the stairs. He too was masked and the stocking had the effect of distorting his voice, like an inaccurately tuned radio. 'Not a sign.'

The man in the hall cocked the shotgun in an increasingly threatening way. 'You're an utter fool, Francis Callaghan, and for what? For the unwanted possessions of a dead man who hated your guts.'

'What about the girl?' the man behind Francis demanded.

'She'll not get far with the front gates locked.'

Joe felt the last glimmer of hope vanish. If the front gates were locked, there was no way Maeve could get out of the estate.

'We'll take care of these beauties first. Then we'll see to her.'

'You'd better not hurt her,' Joe said.

'Kids have no business getting mixed up in what's none of their business.'

'Well, all the same, we are mixed up in it although Callaghan here knew nothing about it,' Dave said.

'Then Callaghan can explain why you'd be best to keep your mouths shut for the next few days.'

'Few days?' The fear in Francis's voice was suddenly unmistakable. 'But the arrangement was ...'

'The arrangements have been changed but not by us. By you. Now come down here.'

Francis needed the support of both Dave and Joe to get down into the hall. The second man kept close behind them. 'Will I get some rope?'

'No. We don't need to tie them up where we're going to put them. Move! Through there!' The man with the shotgun pointed to a close-set door that was almost part of the wall. The second man stepped in front of the procession and held it open. On the other side was a small room that could once have been a sitting-room for a housekeeper. Yet another door opened from it into an enclosed space, like a room without windows. The man with the gun nodded at his companion, who bent down and opened a trapdoor in the floor. Francis made as if to resist but the men pointed the gun directly at Joe. Clearly there was nothing for Francis and Joe and Dave to do except to go down the stone steps into the darkness below. The trap door was dropped into place. At once the darkness became icy cold.

'What is this place?' Dave's face was barely visible as he spoke.

'It's the old storage vaults that were used before there were fridges and deep freezes.'

'And there's no other way out?'

'Not that I know of.'

'Well, let's have a look.'

'No.'

'Why not?'

'Because we'll only make things worse.'

'It's hard to see how things could get any worse than

they are right now,' Dave exclaimed.

'You don't understand,' Francis said.

'Nor will I unless you explain what's going on.'

'It's a long story, that goes back a long way.'

'Back to when you attacked the workman?' Joe asked.

Francis seemed to smile at Joe's words but it was a bitter smile.

'So people still talk about that, do they?'

'Miss Grogan told Maeve. No one else has ever mentioned it.'

'I wish I could believe that.'

'Well it's true,' Dave said. 'I never heard any mention of it either and I have brothers who must be your age. The Brady brothers? Do you remember them?'

'Yes. I was in the same class as Pat.'

'And Brian Costello?' Joe asked.

'Brian and I were the best of friends. Sometimes I think he's the only real friend I ever had.'

'But is it not true that you tried to rob one of the workmen?' Joe could feel the chill of the cellars creep into his bones.

'No, it's not. The fight was over Julia Wiltshaw. You might as well know the truth now just in case things go even more seriously wrong. My father, when he was alive, looked after all the Wiltshaw livestock and, from coming over here with him, I got to know Julia and used to help her with the dogs.'

'We found a photograph of the two of you with Darkie at a dogshow,' Joe said. 'That's how we knew who you were and not because people were still talking about you.'

'It was that photograph that in a way proved our un-

67

doing. Julia and I were doing so well at various shows that we talked about maybe starting a kennels of our own, and then, maybe, when I was qualified as a vet I could set up my practice here, take over from where my father left off. But we had to be very careful that Mr. Wiltshaw didn't find out. He was very possessive about Julia. I suppose he was afraid she might go and leave him by himself in this house. He had no other living relatives. He was also a terrible old snob who thought the people around here were all right to carry out his orders but not really to be treated as humans.' Francis's voice trembled as though the memory of old Mr. Wiltshaw was too much for him.

'He was always nice to Maeve and me,' Joe said.

'Oh yes. He was "nice" to everyone. He probably didn't even think of himself as a snob or a tyrant but that's what he was all the same. It was bred into him to be like that. And there was always the danger that he would disinherit Julia, or at least try to, if he found out that she was becoming too independent.'

'And maybe in love with someone who was not of her class, even though he was the son of a vet?' Dave suggested.

'Yes, that as well, only she and I never spoke of that. But one of the men on the estate, Mick Rourke, who wasn't from these parts at all, somehow got wind of what Julia and I were planning. The picture in the paper started him spying on us. He asked me to meet him out there in the big meadow and what he had to say was very simple and direct. Either Julia and I paid him so much money every week or he'd go to Mr. Wiltshaw with the story of how Julia and I were planning to run away together. I lost my temper with him and hit him. I know it was no solution but I just got so angry. Fortunately Joe Breen saw the row starting and came and separated myself and Mick Rourke. Otherwise I might have done him serious harm.'

'But how did the story of you trying to rob Mick Rourke get out?' Joe tried to picture the scene in the big meadow; Francis towering over the cowardly Mick Rourke, Joe Breen trying to separate them.

'Mick Rourke made the story up to explain why I had attacked him. I kind of stormed off, you see, leaving Mick with Breen. It was only later that I heard what Mick had said. It seemed better for Julia's sake to let that story stand. The funny thing is that everyone, except Brian Costello, believed it.'

'Did Julia believe it as well?'

'No, but Mick Rourke told her he'd go to her father, if she tried to tell the truth.'

'But surely that would be better than having you branded as a thief,' Dave said.

'You don't understand. Julia had no education. All she understood was the estate and the house. She couldn't earn a living away from her home. And I hadn't even got a place at University. Then my mother decided that the people around here would never trust me so she sold up and we moved to Dublin. There seemed to be absolutely nothing myself or Julia or even my mother, when I told her the true story, could do except try and forget. But it's easier to talk about forgetting than to actually forget. Even when I got into the veterinary department at the University, I still found I was thinking about Julia. Then two years ago, I went to a party and

Julia was there. She told me that her father was dead and that she was living in Dublin. She said her life here had been so unhappy for so long that she could no longer bear to live in the place; too many sad memories. But she did ask if I was still interested in starting a kennels. I was and after a few meetings we realized that we still cared about each other and that there was nothing now to prevent us from getting married once I was qualified.

'Then Mick Rourke came back on the scene. It was just one of those things that can happen. Julia and I were walking down the street when suddenly there was Mick Rourke standing in front of us. He behaved as though we were the best of friends. Julia and I couldn't believe our eyes or our ears. We walked away from him. But he followed us. He tried to borrow money from us. We refused. Finally, he went away. We thought that was the end of it. But it wasn't. Two days later, Darkie disappeared. We looked everywhere for him. We told the guards. We put advertisements in the newspapers. We did everything. Then suddenly Darkie was back, sitting on the doorstep with a note tied to his collar. The note said, "Next time Darkie might not be in such good health."'

'And you think Mick Rourke was behind Darkie's disappearance?' Dave asked.

'Who else? But how could we prove it? And Julia was terrified. Weeks passed. Nothing happened. Then some people said they were interested in buying the estate.'

'My father has gone to Dublin to talk to them today.'

'Yes, I know. But something more important happened yesterday than whether or not this place was to be sold. While Julia was out shopping, her flat was broken into and Darkie was taken again. Julia got a message. She could have Darkie back for a hundred pounds. She agreed to be at a certain place at a certain time but by herself. We arranged that she would contact me as soon as she had Darkie back safely. But, when my telephone finally rang, it was not Julia who called but a man, maybe one of those upstairs now, with what he called a "proposition", which was that they needed my co-operation in helping them to take the pick of the rugs and the pictures out of here.'

'Or else something would happen to Julia and the dog?' Dave said.

'Yes. Obviously the men were friends of Mick Rourke. He knew that the way to get to Julia was through Darkie, and to me, through Julia.'

'They'd sent someone down a few weeks back to case the place. Mr. Gallagher told Maeve and me about a stranger, asking if the trees were for sale. That must be when the plan was being formed,' Joe said.

'Yes, that sounds like one of Mick's friends all right although Mick wouldn't have the brains to set up a big deal like this. He'd only be the source of information. He maybe got the idea from stealing Darkie that first time.'

'You should have gone to the guards then,' Dave said.

'I know that now but, at the time, just to get him back safely was enough. There was no way that we could foresee the present situation. Obviously whoever Mick Rourke is in cahoots with has a lot of contacts to be able to sell the stolen goods ...'

'And to know when Julia was going to sell the place?' Dave suggested.

'No, I think that was a coincidence. The real reason today was chosen was because of the outing. Mick Rourke would know about that and how, with the weather so good, everyone that could would be at it. That's why they decided on today.'

'But how did Darkie come to be running around scot-free?'

'I don't know. I came here this morning on the half-baked notion that Julia might actually be held here in the house. I didn't realize that Mr. Gallagher was here until I heard him opening the shutters. I barely had time to duck down behind the urns and somehow I twisted this ankle of mine. But I'd hardly time to feel how painful it was when suddenly there was Darkie beside me.'

'Like out of a dream?' Joe said, remembering the way the dog had startled him and Maeve in the lane.

'Yes, exactly. I grabbed him and managed to keep him quiet while Mr. Gallagher walked down the drive.'

'To see if Brian Costello had left a message.'

'Yes, I knew if I stayed where I was I would be spotted but I knew too I'd never get away from the park-land or even out of sight if Mr. Gallagher came back too soon, so I decided to make for the ditch. I gave Darkie the sign to clear off out of the park.'

'And he thought you wanted him to get help, so when he heard Maeve and me out in the lane, he came to us. But how did he get out of the estate? The meadow gate was bolted and closed.'

'He used the other way out.'

'But which way out was that?'

'The tunnel!'

72

10 The Secret Tunnel

Maeve's heart was beating so fast that she felt that it would burst. 'Joe and Dave! Joe and Dave!' the words bounced through her mind with every step. They were relying on her. For their sake, she had to keep going. 'Oh please,' she prayed, 'don't let Miss Grogan be in one of her fussy moods. Make her let me use the phone without too much talk.'

The line of trees was almost at an end now. Soon she would be obliged to come out into the open but with luck the two men were still searching the house for her.

The main gates were only a few yards ahead of her now. Beyond was the road to Innisdara. A length of chain and a lock were thrown on to the grass by the great stone pillar. Dave had been right about the gate being left open! But even as she reached the gate, Maeve felt a great shock of dismay. There was another lock and chain on the gate; a thick new-looking chain encased in blue plastic.

The men in the black van had replaced the old chain with a new one to prevent any unexpected arrivals from driving up to the house!

Maeve measured herself against the gaps in the bars. She'd never manage to squeeze through them. And neither could she stand there a second longer in the hope that someone might pass by. She could be spotted from the house long before that happened.

She looked around in despair, seeking some

miraculous answer to the terrible problem and there, running towards her, was Darkie, his tail wagging furiously.

'Oh Darkie,' Maeve felt like crying. 'If only you could fly or talk but we mustn't stay here.'

She ran back to the shelter of the trees with Darkie dancing around her, but, as soon as she stood still to try and think, Darkie began to bark furiously. 'Don't, Darkie!' Maeve dropped down and hugged the dog tightly. 'Don't bark! You'll give us away.'

But Darkie was not to be stopped. He broke free as he had done on each previous occasion when anyone tried to detain him. There was about him the same bright-eyed determination as when he had sent the children tumbling into the tip-head fence.

He barked again and clawed at Maeve, his bark dissolving into a series of gentle keens and anguished growls.

'I'm beginning to think that it's all just a great game of chase to you,' Maeve said.

Her voice encouraged Darkie to an even greater outburst of barking. Once more he clawed and ran further back among the trees and then back to her again. 'But there's nothing back there,' Maeve said. Or was there?

Where had the dog come from if not in the direction he was now trying to lead her? And she couldn't be worse off than she was already. 'O.K., Darkie.'

The dog led Maeve towards the wall, utterly confident about where he was going. At a point half-way between the gate and the house, he ploughed into a huge clump of rank weeds and was gone.

Maeve scrambled after him and there on the other

side of a narrow moat-like incline was a short tunnel that went underneath the wall.

Maeve lay on her stomach and wriggled through, to emerge on the edge of a field where a herd of cows gazed at her with great, brown-eyed interest.

Through this field, there was what seemed like a natural fault in the land, but Maeve suddenly realized that the depression was man-made and part of the drainage system that started by the ditch along the drive and led by a series of gentle alterations of ground level to the moat inside a wall and through the tunnel, allowing the water to end up eventually in the canal.

Francis must have used this tunnel to get out of the parkland that morning. As to how he got to the old cottage, that would have to wait until after she got to Innisdara. But Darkie had other views as to which way she should be going. He kept trying to make her change direction until eventually she began to look for a stick to threaten him with.

Yet even when she waved the stick at him, it made no difference to his determination. 'I can't, Darkie! I have to get back to Innisdara.' She reached a gate and started to climb it. Darkie grabbed the end of her jeans. 'Let go, Darkie! No, now, I mean it! Let go!' She pulled free and jumped down on to the road.

Darkie, however, stayed in the field. When Maeve started down the road, the dog ran along on the other side of the hedge, once more barking and keening so anxiously that the possibility that following him might be more important than getting to Innisdara was a thought she could no longer resist.

'All right but only for five minutes.' She could hear

the increase in the dog's speed as he dashed back to watch her climb back over the gate.

He led her through the herd of cows which watched them as calmly as if to see a labrador and a girl run among them was a normal everyday occurence.

Ahead of them was the canal. 'I can't go back across there,' Maeve yelled. 'I just can't, Darkie.' But the dog did not enter the water. Instead, he followed the path, ignoring the cottage and the tip-head over on the other bank, and cutting once more inland across the fields.

Where two fields met there was a squat stone building, used long ago to shelter animals during harsh winter weather. The dog became as still as a statue, not so much listening as seeming to confirm for himself that he was in the right place. Then his tail wagged as Maeve had never seen it wag before and Darkie flung himself against the door.

Maeve undid the wire that held the door shut. Spotlights of sunlight shone through the holes in the roof. The interior smelled of straw and hay. The dust raised by Darkie as he crossed the floor was like a grey snowstorm. Tied and gagged and dumped in a corner was a young woman. Maeve knew that she had to be Julia Wiltshaw!

Maeve quickly removed the gag from Julia's mouth. Julia gasped with relief. 'I was beginning to give up hope. Who are you?'

'Maeve Maguire.'

'Of course, the solicitor's daughter. You've grown so much since I last saw you. Can you undo these ropes?'

It was a difficult task until Maeve realized that there was a pattern to the knots which had to be reversed.

'Good girl!' Julia rubbed her wrists and ankles as she spoke.

'Good Darkie too,' Maeve said. 'He showed me where you were. But we have to get help for the others.'

'What others?' Julia squinted as she stepped out into the sunlight and, for a moment, looked exactly as she did in *The Leinster Leader* photograph.

'Francis and Dave Brady and Joe, my brother; they were caught up at Wiltshaw House. We can phone the guards from Miss Grogan's.'

Julia hesitated. 'All right. I suppose that's the only thing we can do even if it does end up in the newspapers and on television. It's time I stopped thinking of what my father might say about the Wiltshaw name. We can go across to the back road from here, can't we?'

Maeve had forgotten that Julia would of course know her way around the countryside better than even herself and Joe. But Darkie? How did he know the lay of the land so well? He'd surely have only been a pup when he'd left Wiltshaw House.

'Oh I used to come back fairly often without saying a word to anyone and bring Darkie with me. So many people have moved into County Kildare these last few years that strangers are hardly commented on anymore. I suppose I felt guilty about leaving the place locked up but, thank heavens, I did feel that way, otherwise Darkie would never have got to know the lay of the land.'

She glanced at the dog, now contentedly by her side. 'I suppose you could say he was the cause and the answer to all the problems.'

They reached the road which was almost as narrow as

the lane and used only by the Breens for ease of access to the fields furthest from their house. It led away from the canal and the estate, ending up just north of MacGraths' garage on the main street of Innisdara.

'I never thought I'd be so pleased to see this old scrap yard again,' Julia declared as they passed the rear of the premises where for as long as Maeve could remember Mr. McGrath had kept a collection of wrecked vehicles.

'Why do we have to use Miss Grogan's phone?' Julia asked. 'She's a terrible old gossip. Your father surely has a phone.'

'Yes, of course, he does.' Maeve realized there was no real reason to risk being delayed by Miss Grogan. 'We can even go in by the back garden and not be seen at all.'

Darkie followed them into the house and flopped down in the cool kitchen as though he'd lived there for years. Maeve took Julia into the study.

'Maybe you should make the call.'

Julia nodded and picked up the receiver.

'There's no dialling tone.' She jiggled the receiver. 'It seems to be out of order.'

'It can't be,' Maeve said, 'unless ...' She and Julia stared at each other in horror, 'unless the telephone wires into Innisdara have been cut. With everyone so full of the outing, not many people would be using their phones ...'

'And those who tried would never think that it meant that the lines had been deliberately tampered with. Is there a car?'

'There's the Bradys' van. I think Dave said he'd leave it outside their house but I don't know where the keys are.'

78

'Let's look anyway.' They ran out into the street.

Miss Grogan's curtains were jerked back, and by the time Julia and Maeve had reached the Bradys' van, Miss Grogan was hurrying down the street after them.

'Well, well, if it isn't Julia Wiltshaw. I didn't know you were back. What's going on?'

'I'm sorry but there's no time for explanations now.'

'But Maeve and Joe are in my care. Their parents said I was to look after ...' If the next word was to be 'them', it never got spoken for a motor bike roared down the street and screeched to a stop in front of them. 'Brian Costello!' Miss Grogan's mouth fell wide open. 'I never knew you had a motor bike.'

Brian ignored Miss Grogan and spoke directly to Julia. 'Are you all right?'

'Yes, Maeve found me. But the others are being held prisoners up at the house ...'

'Held prisoners ...?' Miss Grogan's voice was definitely wobbly.

'And we think the telephone lines have been cut ...'

'Telephone lines cut ...?' Miss Grogan's eyes rolled back as though she were hearing disembodied voices.

'We were going to use the Bradys' van but we don't know where the keys are.'

'Usually they leave them under the front seat. Do you know where the Bradys are building the new bungalow?' Julia nodded to Brian's question. 'Go and get Dave's brothers and meet us at the front gates of Wiltshaw House.'

Julia opened the door of the van and found the keys. Brian was already on his way to McGraths' garage. 'I'm going to get the keys for the school bus. In fact you could call me a key-figure around here!' He grinned at his own joke.

'I'm coming with you,' Maeve declared.

'You most certainly are not,' Miss Grogan said.

'I know a secret way into the grounds. I have to go.'

Brian took a bunch of keys off a hook inside the door of the garage.

Maeve said, 'Are you sure you can drive it?'

'Of course. I used to drive lorries for a living at one time.'

Miss Grogan stood dazed in the middle of the street while the van and the bus roared off. 'What will I tell Mr. and Mrs. Maguire when they get back?'

A black streak passed her giving her yet another fright. It was Darkie, determined that he wouldn't be left behind either.

Maeve said to Brian, 'Are you really a key figure? Or was that just a joke?'

'A serious joke,' Brian said seriously. 'Francis Callaghan and I have always remained good friends. I'd see him whenever I went to Dublin and I knew that he and Julia wanted to get married. Then the thieves snatched Julia and Darkie, and Francis decided he had no choice but to co-operate with the plan to rob Wilt-shaw House. I met him by chance this morning after he'd hurt his foot. That's when I got involved; just before you and Joe started following him!'

'It was really Darkie who did the following. We just tried to keep up and discover what was going on. But how was it that Darkie was on the loose like that if the crooks had taken him?'

'I don't know.'

'Well, how did Francis get back to the cottage so quickly after we first saw him at Wiltshaw House?'

'I took him there.'

'You did?'

'Yes, on the motor bike. I stopped to leave a message for Mr. Gallagher and was going on to the Breens when I saw the motor bike parked under a hedge. Next minute, Francis came limping out of the field.'

'So he had used the tunnel to both get in and out of the parkland. But why didn't Darkie show us that way instead of the meadow gate?'

'Maybe he was going to, only Joe used the meadow gate. We'd have used it as well if we'd known it was unlocked.'

'So Francis didn't remove the lock. Mr. Gallagher simply forgot to put it back when he arrived home last night. That's when Joe and I got so confused and worried at the thought of some intruder around the place.'

Brian grinned again. 'You mean you aren't still worried and confused?'

'Oh yes. I'm very worried. One of the thieves has a gun and the main gates are locked with a new chain and lock.'

Brian's grin faded. 'What are you talking about?'

'The old lock and chain are thrown on the grass inside the gate. There's one of those plastic chains on the gate instead. But the tools? What about those burglar tools?'

'I lost them.'

'And we found them. They could still be in Dave's van.' Maeve looked quickly at Brian. 'Why did you need those anyway?'

'Part of the great plan. If Francis used keys to get into the place, the guards would suspect an inside job and the story about Francis trying to rob Mick Rourke would be dragged out into the open. So Francis was told to cut the chain off the main gate. Of course I now realize that if Francis had cut the chains, it would look as though he was actually part of the gang.'

'I'm sure Miss Grogan would believe that. Maybe Mr. Gallagher as well.'

'It's called giving a dog a bad name. And speaking of dogs, where's Darkie?'

'With Julie, I suppose.' Maeve felt both sad and happy as she said this. The happiness was because Julia and Darkie had been safely reunited. The sadness was because she had been half hoping Darkie might end up belonging to herself and Joe.

The school bus was just a few yards from the main gates of Wiltshaw House now.

'It could have been made for the job,' Brian said. 'Just the right length for blocking the gate. I don't think we should cut the new chain off the gate and drive up to the house if, as you think, one of the men has a gun.'

Maeve agreed. Then a new question came to her.

'You said "if" Francis had cut the chains, he'd be accused of being part of the gang. But if Francis didn't cut them, then who did?'

'I did, of course,' Brian said.

11 Darkie to the Rescue

A familiar cloud of dust was rattling down the road. It was the Bradys' van with Julia still driving and Dave's brothers in the back. Maeve had forgotten how big they were. They looked like a football team determined to win an All-Ireland medal, no matter what it involved.

'We are going to use the tunnel,' Brian said, 'and we'll need to be very careful. Maeve thinks one of the men has a gun. They also think that Maeve is still hiding in the grounds. That at least may work to our advantage.'

The Brady brothers nodded but, when they got to the tunnel, it was obvious that the two eldest were far too big to get through. 'We'll shin up the wall,' Pat said to the second eldest, Simon, which they did with amazing ease for two such big men.

Maeve went through the tunnel first. Then Julia. Then Brian. Then Des and Willie Brady.

Pat said, 'We'll go in different directions and surround the house but we have to stay in among the trees until Maeve has lured the villains out of the house.'

'And how do you think she is going to do that?' Julia asked.

'Just by walking up the drive.'

Maeve stepped out into the open at the point closest to the main gates and started towards the house. She reached the point where Francis had been hiding in the ditch. Everything was again still and out of time. Then the hall door opened and the two masked men came out.

'So you finally came back, did you? Realized you were locked in?'

Maeve kept on walking towards them.

'Well you can keep the others company down in the cellar.'

'THE CELLAR! THE CELLAR!' Maeve screeched the words as loud as she could. They echoed around and around the parkland so that everyone hiding among the trees could hear.

'Hey, cut that out!' The men came quickly down the steps. Maeve focussed her whole being on the open door behind them and flung herself forward, catching the men off balance and jumping into the hall. She slammed the hall door and banged the bolt into place.

Where could the cellar be?

'Joe! Joe! Where are you?'

A muffled shout came from the darkness of a room she had never seen before.

'Joe! Joe!'

The voices that answered were from underneath the floor, but before she could discover the trapdoor she was grabbed from behind and swung into the air like a sack of potatoes. 'You forgot you opened the back door when you left!'

Maeve struggled but the man just laughed. 'But you won't be joining the others after all. You're coming with us instead. Your friends, unfortunately, like you, forgot there are two doors into the house and came out of hiding too soon.'

The man carried Maeve across the kitchen and into the yard. She caught a quick glimpse of Julia and Brian, their hands raised as the second man pointed the sawn-

off shotgun at them. 'No foolishness now, please.'
Maeve was tossed in on top of a heap of rolled-up rugs.
The back doors of the van were slammed and the van

sped out of the yard and around the side of the house on to the drive.

The man at the wheel swore. 'They've blocked the gate with a bus. Keep an eye on the girl.' He got out of the van and unlocked the chain on the gate and pulled the gates open. 'We'll never fit past here. Still, those that block things can unblock them. Take the girl out of the van.'

Maeve was hauled roughly out on to the ground. As she managed to stand up, she saw the Bradys standing in a group a short distance away. Running down the drive were Julia and Brian. Behind them, trying to keep up, for the cold of the cellar had chilled their muscles, were Dave and Joe and Francis.

'Whoever parked that bus can unpark it or else your young friend here suffers.'

'Darkie!' It was hard to tell whether Julia called the name as a warning or a command as Darkie launched himself through the open gates at the man with the key. The dog's weight knocked the man over. The second man suddenly didn't know what to do. He pointed the gun away from the onlookers and then at Darkie as the dog plonked himself on top of the first man. 'Are you crazy?' the trapped man cried. 'If you miss the dog, you could hit me!'

Maeve drew her foot back as far as she could and aimed it as hard as she could at the gunman's shin. The effect was amazing as he jumped in the air and dropped the gun. Maeve kicked the weapon well out of his reach. As if from a distance, she heard Dave say, 'Terrific! Just like a Clint Eastwood film.' Then she was surrounded by Julia and Joe and Dave. Everything was grand again.

12 Tea at Miss Grogan's

'Well, I never heard the like, never, never!' declared Miss Grogan, looking at them all crowded into her front room, drinking tea, 'although I don't understand the half of it.'

'It's really quite simple,' Joe said. 'First Darkie was taken and then Julia to make sure that Francis would follow instructions. Francis came down to see if Julia was hidden anywhere around here and hurt his foot trying to avoid Mr. Gallagher. That's when Darkie first showed up, and Maeve and I saw Francis in the ditch.'

'And I couldn't take a chance on being stopped and questioned so I got back to the tunnel as quick as I could with Darkie.' Francis had his injured foot propped up on a footstool. Julia was on the sofa next to him. Darkie, at Miss Grogan's insistence, had been left in the Maguires' back garden with a bone and a bowl of water. 'Fortunately Brian saw the motor bike in the hedge. Otherwise, I'd never have been able to use it. He took me back to the cottage by the canal. Mick Rourke had recommended that to the thieves as a good place to contact me and to leave the tools to cut the chains on the main gate. I was also told to stay there until tomorrow morning. That's why I needed the sleeping-bag '

'And why could they not have cut the chains themselves?' Miss Grogan demanded, as though it was a sign of deliberate laziness on the part of the criminals.

'Brian says it was so that they could claim that Francis

was a crook as well.'

'Well people love to think the worst,' Miss Grogan said.

'Will they think the worst of me when they hear I was the one who did the cutting?' Brian Costello asked mischievously.

But Miss Grogan thought there was nothing funny about the idea. Anyway, she wanted to get the story straight so that she could repeat it to all her friends. 'After you got back to the cottage? What then?' She began to pour more tea. 'You left Darkie behind you at the tunnel. Yet Maeve and Joe found him at the cottage.'

'No, he was at the tip-head,' Maeve corrected her. 'Joe and I almost figured it out but not quite. There's the old sand quarry behind the tip-head and you can get from the quarry to the cottage without going out on to the road. The black van that turned up at Wiltshaw House must have been parked there. We saw the tyre marks.'

'And I was in the van,' Julia almost laughed as Miss Grogan's eyes widened even more. 'You see they drove me down in it last night along with Darkie and kept us both in the cowshed. It's never used this time of year so they knew it was safe. But this morning when they opened the door, Darkie got out. Maybe they thought they'd be better off without him. Every time they moved he barked and they were afraid of him, in spite of having a gun. But they knew all the same that if Francis saw Darkie he might follow him back to the shed, so they took me out of the shed back into the van and waited all morning in the old quarry.'

'So, in fact at one time for a few minutes, we were all within a few yards of each other?' Maeve said.

'Yes. Darkie couldn't keep up with the motor cycle when Brian drove me off on it from the tunnel,' Francis said, 'so he went back for the two of you but, before he got to you, he heard us coming along the canal road and must have doubled back towards the sound and swum across.'

'And at the same time, Julia was being driven into the quarry in the van, so Darkie didn't know which way to go until you two got to the canal bank,' Brian said. 'Francis and I were watching you. Darkie knew by then he could trust you so he waited for you.'

'Even in the van, I could hear him barking,' Julia said. 'It gave the two thieves such a fright that they drove off. The scooped-out hill in the quarry absorbed sounds so only Darkie heard the van leave to dump me back in the cowshed before the robbery took place.'

'And by the time we got to the quarry, the van was gone and so were Brian and Francis out of the cottage on the motor bike to Naas,' Maeve said.

'It seemed too risky to stay in the cottage,' Francis said. 'We didn't know what you would decide to do and my foot was so bad by then that I knew if I didn't put a bandage on it, I wouldn't be able to walk at all. The rest you know ...'

'All except for Brian. Why did Brian come back to the cottage?' Dave, who had been listening as intently as Miss Grogan, spoke for the first time in ages.

'The tools. We forgot the tools that Mick Rourke's friends had left in the cottage for Francis to cut the chain on the gate. I had to come back for them and I lost them

89

so I had to come and borrow more out of McGraths' garage. In fact, I have a lot of explaining to do to Mr. McGrath, not only about the tools but about the bus as well.'

'And my motor bike is still in the middle of the road.' Francis eased himself off the sofa with a grimace of pain.

'You can't go on a motor bike with your sore foot,' Miss Grogan said. 'A hurt like that needs seeing to.'

'Oh it'll be all right till the morning. And anyway, I can be the passenger and Julia can do the driving.'

'Julia Wiltshaw, you haven't taken to rushing around on motor bikes!' Miss Grogan seemed more shocked by that than by anything else she had heard.

'What about Darkie?' Maeve asked hopefully. 'He could stay with us for a few days if you like.' Then, carefully avoiding Joe's eyes, she added, 'I'm sure Dad and Mam wouldn't mind. After all, it's an emergency.'

But Miss Grogan hadn't been given nearly enough information. 'Now you've done enough rushing around for one day and you haven't finished the story. Where was Francis when Brian borrowed the tools out of McGraths?'

'I was waiting with the bike in the laneway where Darkie met Maeve and Joe. Brian cut the chains on the gate and I went up to the house to wait for the black van to arrive. They wanted me there while they were stealing the things. I thought it was in case I called the guards but really it was to involve me even further if anything went wrong.'

'But how did you get into the house?' Miss Grogan demanded.

'I broke a window in the scullery. After I opened the

front door, I got worried in case Mr. Gallagher had changed his mind about the outing. I went upstairs to check his bedroom and was resting my foot when Maeve and Joe and Dave found me.'

Miss Grogan looked at Brian. 'And you?'

'I'd stayed out of sight until I was sure Innisdara was deserted before coming back on the motor bike with the tools to McGraths. I couldn't believe my eyes when I saw Julie standing in the street with you. The only trouble is that I seem to have lost the McGraths' tools as well.'

'Oh well, I'm sure they can easily be replaced,' Miss Grogan began to collect the empty cups. 'The main thing is that the guards have those two men under lock and key. And of course that Julia is safe. Now I think a poem might be nice before supper,'

'But we've just had tea.' Joe had a sudden urge to leave.

'Oh now, a cup of tea and a few sandwiches is not enough after what you've been through. A nice poem will calm us all down. Joe reads poetry beautifully,' Miss Grogan said to Julia as she reached for the book on the mantlepiece. 'The one about *Golden Evenings* would do very nicely.'

There was no way out. Joe took the open book and began to read:

> *Golden days do golden evenings give*
> *As all things that live*
> *Sigh at the peaceful end of day ...*

Joe's voice filled the room and he no longer felt embarrassed. It seemed like a good thing to be doing.

Outside the street had lost its bright light and was now various shades of grey and blue. The school bus was back in place. People, returning from the outing, went into Mr. Kelly's pub and heard of the extraordinary happenings at Wiltshaw House and how the Maguire children had been responsible for two men being arrested and, maybe, even a whole gang dealing in stolen antiques being exposed.

Mr. Gallagher was inclined to be cross at what he considered undue interference with his right to dictate what happened at Wiltshaw House but then, when he put his hand in his jacket pocket and found the lock that he had forgotten to put back on the meadow gate, he decided it was best to say nothing.

Joe finished the poem. Maeve couldn't avoid a yawn.

'You should be in bed,' Miss Grogan said.

'It's only half-past six,' Maeve said. 'And we have to tell Mam and Dad the full story. Julia will want to talk to them as well. After all, she was supposed to meet them in Dublin today.'

'I only hope that when the story of the attempted robbery gets out those people won't change their minds about buying the estate,' Julia said.

'Oh but you're not still going to sell,' Maeve protested. 'Just as everything is turning out so well.'

'There are just too many unhappy memories associated with the place. Anyway, it's far too big for us. We'll look for somewhere in Wicklow or Wexford, far enough away to start a new life, yet close enough for our friends to visit us. And I hope you'll all do that.'

'Of course we will,' declared Miss Grogan as though Julia had been particularly thinking of her.

'Let's go and see how Darkie is,' Maeve said to Joe.

They found some dry sacks for him to sleep on and then sat with him on the back door steps watching the shadows creep across the garden.

'We never found Finn's Way,' Maeve said.

'There's always tomorrow.' Joe stroked Darkie's head.

The whole sky was ablaze with the reds and scarlets and orange of the setting sun as Mr. and Mrs. Maguire left the motorway on the last stretch of the homeward journey. Mr. Maguire was in a terrible mood after a whole day spent in the city waiting for Julia Wiltshaw although the peace of the countryside soon had a soothing effect on him.

Mrs. Maguire said, 'I hope the children weren't too bored trailing around the countryside by themselves.'

'At their age, they've no right to be bored. I just hope they won't start that business about wanting a dog again.'

'What put that in your mind?'

'I don't know.'

A squad car, siren blazing, came towards them.

'I wonder what brought them out?' Mrs. Maguire turned and looked after it.

'Nothing to do with us, I'll bet,' Mr. Maguire said with great confidence.

Notes for Teachers

County Kildare, although lacking a prehistoric site as dramatic as Newgrange, has, like neighbouring Meath, a history rich in folklore and legend, from the prehistory associations with the Fianna at the Hill of Allen and Kilcullen to later Christian associations with St. Brigid and the miraculous creation of the Curragh and the convent at Kildare through the spreading of her cloak.

The town of Naas was a trading centre of great importance from earliest times, especially famous for its horse fairs, an activity which must to a certain extent have dictated the width of its main street. A similar consideration must also have affected the development of Newbridge, where cattle and horse fairs were held very regularly, until the 1950s, on its main street.

The breeding of horses on the great limestone plain would have been an important factor in the growth of the county of Kildare as a settled community. This continues to be true today. The area is the centre of Ireland's great bloodstock industry, and all the classic races, including the Irish Derby, one of Europe's most prestigious races, are run at the Curragh racecourse.

The river Liffey also played its part in the establishment of early settlements. The town of Newbridge which, as its name implies, was a place where the river was easily crossed, giving access to the Curragh, made it an ideal base for garrisons, probably from very early times.

The building of the canal system was also vital to the

development of the county. Robertstown, once a bustling port of call on the Grand Canal, has a superb canal hotel, preserved through the efforts of the local people.

Fringing the valuable agricultural land is the great Bog of Allen, which has played such a vital part in the economy of modern Ireland, both as a source of fuel for domestic and power stations, as well as producing by-products for the horticultural and plastic industries.

The Black Dog, in addition to telling an exciting story, is also designed to arouse interest in the area in which it is set, an area ideal for school outings, close to many large centres of population, with an excellent road system.

Some suggested projects: The Fianna in County Kildare; the spread of Christianity; the Curragh as a garrison centre; the importance of the bloodstock industry to Ireland; the economic and environmental importance of the bog; the changing face of travel, from canal to motorway.

Tony Hickey

Tony Hickey was born in Newbridge, County Kildare, where he grew up.

After a time spent in educational film-making and radio and TV drama, he first began writing for children in the BBC's *Jackanory* programme and RTE's *Story-room*. He also worked on *An Baile Beag* and *Wanderly Wagon*, and has dramatized several children's classics for radio including *The Wizard of Oz*, *The Lost Prince* and Patricia Lynch's autobiography, *A Storyteller's Childhood*, which is also published by The Children's Press. He is at present working on the pilot of a new TV series and on a radio play for Radio Eireann.

The Black Dog, set in the countryside of his boyhood, will be the first, we hope, of many stories about the Maguires and the little town of Innisdara. He has also written *The Matchless Mice* and *The Matchless Mice's Adventure*, both with illustrations by Pauline Bewick.